08·16

DATE DUE

THE WOMEN OF THE SOUK

A Mamur Zapt Mystery

Michael Pearce

This first world edition published 2016
in Great Britain and the USA by
SEVERN HOUSE PUBLISHERS LTD of
19 Cedar Road, Sutton, Surrey, England, SM2 5DA.
Trade paperback edition first published
in Great Britain and the USA 2016 by
SEVERN HOUSE PUBLISHERS LTD

British Library Cataloguing in Publication Data
A CIP catalogue record for this title is available from the British Library.

ISBN-13: 978-0-7278-8618-7 (cased)
ISBN-13: 978-1-84751-719-7 (trade paper)
ISBN-13: 978-1-78010-780-6 (e-book)

All Severn House titles are printed on acid-free paper.

Severn House Publishers support the Forest Stewardship Council™ [FSC™],
the leading international forest certification organisation.
All our titles that are printed on FSC certified paper carry the FSC logo.

MIX
Paper from
responsible sources
FSC
www.fsc.org   FSC® C013056

Typeset by Palimpsest Book Production Ltd.,
Falkirk, Stirlingshire, Scotland.
Printed and bound in Great Britain by
TJ International, Padstow, Cornwall.

ONE

The slats on the shutters were heavy with sand this morning. He opened and closed them a few times to shake the sand off. It was then that he noticed the girl. He went back to his desk. When he looked out again she was still standing there.

'That girl,' he said to his official clerk.

'Girl?' said Nikos.

'In the yard. How long has she been standing there?'

Nikos peered at her, as if seeing her for the first time.

'About a couple of hours,' he said indifferently.

'A couple of hours? Christ!'

Immediately he had said that, he felt guilty. Nikos was a Copt, and therefore a Christian. In Cairo, with its explosive mixture of races and religions, you didn't take these things lightly.

'Two hours at least!' said Nikos with satisfaction. He didn't believe in girls.

'But why? What is she doing there?'

'Waiting to see you.'

'Waiting to . . .? Look – I thought I had given explicit instructions that no one—'

'She's only a schoolgirl,' said Nikos dismissively.

'Schoolgirls too.'

Nikos shrugged. There was no end to the Mamur Zapt's eccentricities.

'Tell her to come in!'

Nikos got up from his desk, huffily, and went out. A few moments later the girl came in.

'Captain Owen!' she said, a little nervously but determinedly, and not in Arabic nor in the usual French of the Egyptian upper classes, but in English.

'How can I help?'

'It is about Marie.'

'Marie?'

'There,' said the girl. 'You don't even know about her!'

'Ought I to?'

'You're the Chief of Police, aren't you?'

'No,' said Owen. 'I'm the Head of the Special Branch. I deal only with political matters.'

'This is a political matter.'

'What exactly is the problem?'

'She's disappeared. And no one is doing anything about it.'

'Presumably it has been reported to the police? The ordinary police, that is.'

'Yes. And they told me to bugger off.'

'I'm sorry about that. They shouldn't have done that.'

She toyed nervously with the hem of her dress and now, he took it in, he saw that she wasn't wearing the traditional dark, full-length burka but a modern school girl's uniform. And no veil.

'You're at the Khedivial,' he said.

The Khedivial Girls' School, newly set up, was where the top civil servants sent their daughters.

'Yes. I'm in the seniors. What you would call the sixth form.'

This probably accounted for the poise with which she was addressing him. In Egypt at that time women did not normally address men directly but through a masculine intermediary, usually a male relative. And young girls did not address men at all.

'Perhaps I shouldn't have spoken to them the way I did,' she admitted, 'but I was so angry when they treated me like that.'

'How did you speak to them?'

'I told them to bugger off themselves and find me someone more senior.'

'And?'

'They threw me out.'

Owen laughed.

'It is not a laughing matter,' she said. 'Just because I'm a woman. They treat women like dirt.'

'I'm sorry I laughed. I shouldn't have done. I meant to have expressed approval.'

'Really?'

He nodded.

She was silent for a moment. Then she said: 'I expect it's because of Zeinab.'

'You know about Zeinab?' he said, surprised.

'All the world knows about you and Zeinab!'

Owen hoped they didn't.

'You don't know how much we admire her, Captain Owen! To have the strength to go against everyone, to go your own way, to shape out a life for yourself! She is a model to us all!'

'Us?'

'All Egyptian women and especially the sixth form at the Khedivial.'

'Look—'

'She is an example of the New Woman. We know all about the New Woman, Captain Owen. We read the French newspapers daily, and occasionally the English ones, though I think they're feeble. Don't you, Captain Owen? They're so pompous, so . . . male! The French ones are better. They are setting out the new styles. The New Women. Don't you think that's very important, Captain Owen? The world is changing and women are changing it. Or, perhaps, they will change it. And we will be at the forefront, Captain Owen, we won't be lagging behind!'

'I'm sure you won't but—'

'We are prepared to suffer. Like the suffragettes. We read the English newspapers too, and the thing is, you see, Zeinab has set an example!'

'Look, I'm not sure she would recognise herself in quite that role.'

'And we think you're very brave to go along with her to the extent you do. Of course we realise how difficult it must be for you. We do appreciate it, Captain Owen, believe me – actually, that's the reason why they sent me to see you. They thought that you were in a position to get something done and would be sympathetic. At first we thought of going direct to Zeinab but we thought that what with the baby and all that she's got enough on her hands already.'

'You know about the baby?'

'We're pretty well-informed. I must say, I don't think we should get on to the baby questions just yet, though. These traditional tasks should still take second place in Egypt, at least for the time being. But we've got to do something about Marie. It may already be too late. If she really has been kidnapped.'

'Kidnapped?'

'That is what we think has happened to her.'

'Have you any grounds for supposing this?'

'Oh yes,' she said, 'oh yes.'

Over her shoulder he could see Nikos looking at him reproach-fully and tapping the big bundle of papers under his arm.

He ignored him.

'First, your name.'

'Layla.'

'And you're at the Khedivial and Marie is one of your classmates?'

'Yes.'

'What is her name? Her full name?'

'Kewfik. Marie Kewfik.'

And suddenly it became plausible. Kewfik was one of the biggest names in Egypt. There were Kewfiks at court, Kewfiks all through the government.

'What makes you think she has been kidnapped?'

'She hasn't been to school for over a week now and when we went to her home and asked about her, they wouldn't say anything.'

'Perhaps she's ill.'

'No. We asked her maid and she isn't ill.'

'Gone away?'

'Why wouldn't the maid tell us if she's just gone away? And why wouldn't Marie have told us? She tells us everything. She's a great chatterbox, and, anyway, you can't go away. Not in term time. It is one of the things the school is very strict about. When it started people were always drifting off, if they wanted to have a picnic or something like that. But the Head put her foot down and got the fathers to put *their* feet down. And the mothers, who had always been pretty soft, had to do what they said. Even my mother, who usually doesn't take any notice of what my father says. "I have to go to work every day," he said, "So why shouldn't she?"'

'And then one day Marie didn't turn up. You told the teachers presumably?'

'We have a roll call every morning and when Marie wasn't

there, the teacher said: "Where is Marie?" and then she went off and reported it at the office and presumably told the Head because when she came back she said: "Forget about it! Got that? Just keep quiet about it!" So of course we knew that something had happened to her.

'Well, individually we asked all the teachers but none of them would say a thing. Well, then we asked the servants, because girls are brought to school, you know. But they wouldn't say anything either. And the worst thing was that they seemed scared. They weren't just keeping their mouths shut because they had been told to. They were actually frightened. They wouldn't say anything at all.

'I went to see the Head and she said it was none of my business, and that I was to keep out of it. So I said: "Is Marie all right?" and she said she hoped so. Well, that wasn't much of an answer, was it? So we asked around some more. We even went to the hospitals in case she had had an accident. And of course, everyone was talking to their parents and there was the same reaction everywhere, nobody would say anything. We got people to ask their fathers, and it was just the same. As soon as they heard the name Kewfik they just backed off. Not as far as my father had done, he is chicken-livered, but they just didn't want to hear!'

'So then you went to the police?'

'We would have gone before but the Head said, "Just keep right out of it! Right out!" So we did. I did. But then when nothing seemed to be happening and Marie still wasn't there, I decided to go myself. I thought I would insist on talking to the Head of Police, that funny old Scotsman, who's quite nice when you talk to him. But they wouldn't let me talk to him, and, well, you know the rest of the story. Maybe I shouldn't have spoken the way I did, but somebody's got to do something, haven't they?

'At the beginning we thought she might have caught scarlet fever or something, and that the school might be closed, and we could all stay at home. I even went round to the Kewfiks' house, I often go there, I'm a friend of Marie, and I thought I might ask her mother directly, but when I got there I could hear her crying in an inside room. It was awful! I knew there must be something very wrong, so I didn't like to ask.

'And then one of the girls said: "You know why they're not

saying anything? She must have been kidnapped and they're negotiating the ransom and everyone has been told to keep off."

'We thought at first that this was just schoolgirl talk, but she insisted. She said she had once been involved in something like this, actually, she hadn't been but you know how girls like to make it big. A cousin of hers had disappeared and everyone had been told to keep quiet about it while the police were conducting their investigation – but, actually all the time the family were negotiating a ransom. The police didn't want anyone to talk about it. The family didn't, but the kidnappers panicked and one day her cousin was found with her throat cut.

'That's what she said, anyway. It was probably all talk, but you can imagine how it made us feel! And we thought that there might be something in it, because there seemed to be a general conspiracy of silence. People were refusing to answer our questions, and the clinching thing was her mother crying! It was awful!

'So I decided to get to the bottom of it, and – well, you know, I thought of going to Zeinab first because she's a woman and would understand. But then we thought we shouldn't do that because she's got so much on her hands and someone suggested why not go direct to you? You couldn't be totally stupid if you're married to Zeinab. Of course, you may not actually be married, but that is no concern of mine, as our Head would probably say, and I accept it's not my business, and, anyway, we're all pretty broad-minded in the seniors, in fact, we believe in freedom in such things, a woman should be free to make up her own mind – but meanwhile, there's poor Marie. Heaven knows what is happening to her! You will help us, won't you, Mamur Zapt?'

These things happened in Egypt; not as often as in the past, but too often and they were not easy to handle. If you gave in and paid the ransom, it would encourage others to do likewise. But if you held out – and it was very difficult for a family to hold out – what often happened was that the kidnappers panicked and killed the unfortunate whom they had seized. Whatever you did was wrong. The police hated such cases.

And it was entirely possible that this was what had happened. The Kewfiks were a rich family and a prime target.

And if it had happened, what would follow was exactly what the schoolgirl had described: a thick veil of silence would fall over everybody.

Owen was too old a hand, however, to assume on a schoolgirl's word that it was the case. He would do some checking first. He sat her in a comfortable chair, passed her a glass of water from the earthenware jug which stood perpetually as in all Cairo offices on his desk, gave strict instructions to a sulky Nikos that she was on no account to be disturbed, and went next door to a phone where he could speak confidentially.

The first person he phoned was McPhee, the Chief of the City Police.

'Yes, it's true,' McPhee said at once. 'Kewfik's daughter has been kidnapped. We've not seen a note yet but it's pretty clear that's what has happened. The matter is complicated by the fact her father has had a stroke and is out of it all completely. His brother is handling everything.'

'So there are negotiations?'

'The beginning of. We haven't got far as yet.'

'The beginning is always the most difficult.'

'Part of the problem is the brother, the girl's uncle, Ali Fingari,' said McPhee. 'He is quite elderly – the senior brother – and I'm not sure he is the man for this.'

'Could you take over the negotiations yourself?'

'I'm not sure I'm the man, either,' said McPhee.

He was, unfortunately, almost certainly right. He was honest, decent and utterly straightforward, admirable qualities in themselves but not at all helpful in Cairo.

'Are you thinking of taking a hand yourself?' said McPhee hopefully.

'No, no. I'm involved only tangentially.'

'A pity,' said McPhee. 'These things are not for me.'

'They're not for anybody really. It's a pity about the uncle.'

'He's an ex-soldier. One of the old school. A bit of a martinet. Which doesn't help in the present situation. He has the whole household running around, but they're only running in circles, and he's no help at all to poor Mrs Kewfik.'

'You've spoken to her?'

'She's more or less collapsed. It's as if he's blamed the incident

on her, for not bringing her daughter up properly. As if it's her
fault.'

'For negotiations of this sort you need to be a bit supple.'

'Supple,' said McPhee, 'is what he definitely is not! My guess
is that he talks to the negotiators as if they were his private
soldiers. His to command.'

'That will get him nowhere.'

'Worse than that,' said McPhee. 'Think of how it might turn
out for the poor girl at the end of all this!'

It was the kind of remark that endeared McPhee to Owen. It
drove other people mad. It was generally said that McPhee was
too tender-hearted for his own good. He should have been put
out to pasture years before.

He was certainly different from the usual colonial policeman.
Most of them were ex-soldiers. McPhee had his uses, however.
He was able to talk to elderly Egyptian women, a skill which very
few people possessed. An old dear talking to old dears, his friend
Paul had once said unkindly. But sometimes you needed people
like that. Such as now, when it might be handy to have someone
who could talk to Mrs Kewfik and bypass the martinet brother.

Owen went back to his room, where the girl was still sitting.
She looked up at him hopefully.

'It is as you supposed,' he said gently. 'Your friend has been
kidnapped.'

'Oh!' she gasped, and shrank back visibly.

'The good thing is she is still alive. Not only that: they appear
to have opened negotiations and while they are continuing Marie
should, I think, be safe.'

She sat for a moment taking this in, then she said: 'Who is
conducting the negotiations?'

'On Marie's side, her uncle.'

'That is a pity,' she said. 'I don't think he likes Marie.'

'Is that a personal thing?'

'I don't think he likes women generally. But he certainly
doesn't like young girls like Marie. He thinks they are too forward,
immodest. I spoke to him once, just to ask if he had seen Marie
– we were in the Kewfiks' house, it's a big one and I didn't know
my way around, and had lost her – and he glared at me as if I

had done something awful, just by speaking to him. He didn't answer, just walked straight past, and I'm pretty sure he's like that with Marie. Once she spoke to him about something minor and he snapped at her and then complained to her mother. I heard all this and was amazed! I don't think there is anything personal in it, it's just the way he is with women.'

'It ought not affect the negotiations anyway.'

'No.'

She seemed doubtful, however.

'It may be taken out of his hands,' Owen said.

'That would be best.'

She stood up, then hesitated.

'Do you think it would be all right if I sent Mrs Kewfik a letter, saying we were all thinking of her?'

'I don't see why you shouldn't. Although, of course, no one is supposed to know.'

'I needn't say anything about the kidnapping. I can just say we're sorry Marie's been away and hope she comes back soon.'

'That would be best, I think.'

He thought for a moment.

'Could the letter be sent through some neutral person, who wouldn't raise the uncle's hackles?'

'Hackles?'

Although her English was good, this was a new one on her.

'Make him cross.'

'Anything makes him cross! But I know what you mean. I can send it through Aimée's mother. She's great friends with Marie's mother.'

'That sounds a good idea.'

She put her hand out.

'And thank you very much, Captain Owen. It has been very kind of you.'

'Not at all.'

'The thing is she *must* still be alive.'

'And where there's life,' said Owen, 'there's hope.'

'I know that one,' she said.

She had hardly left the room when Owen heard his phone go in the outer office. It was from the Consul-General's Assistant who was a particular friend of Owen's. They worked closely together and between them managed to forestall a lot of problems which would otherwise have landed on the Consul-General's desk. As possibly now.

'Gareth,' said Paul, 'have you heard about Kewfik's daughter?'

'Only that she has been kidnapped. I hope there have been no nasty developments?'

'Not yet as far as I know. They're still negotiating. That's what I want to talk to you about. The family has been on to the Khedive apparently. They're not happy about the way things are going.'

'McPhee says that negotiations are being handled on the family side by an elderly uncle who's not up to the mark.'

'The Khedive says that, too. But he also says that the police aren't up to it either.'

'McPhee, you mean?'

'Yes.'

'Well, there's something to be said for that point of view.'

'The Old Man thinks that too, he reckons that McPhee is out of his depth.'

'Very probably.'

'They've put their heads together, the Khedive and the Old Man, and they feel that the thing to do is take it out of the hands of the pair of them, the uncle and McPhee.'

'I can see the logic.'

'And get it handled by someone else.'

'I don't like the sound of this!'

'You're right: the obvious person is you.'

'I don't think so.'

'The Old Man would be happier that way, and the Khedive would not be unhappy. If things went wrong, the British could be blamed. There's a snag though.'

'Just the one?'

'The uncle . . . he's not willing. He wants to keep in control.'

'One of those, is he?'

'Yes, and there's a further consideration: money.'

'Money?'

'The uncle doesn't want to pay out just for a girl. Now a boy might be different. And as it happens, the uncle's got a son. In the uncle's view, he's just the chap for the job. Although apparently, in no one else's.'

'What is the father's attitude?'

'Curiously, the father favours his daughter. Or so the mother says. The uncle says she's not to be trusted. She's a woman. But there's some evidence that the father loves his daughter. There! What a strange thing in an Egyptian family! Unfortunately, for the daughter, the father is out of it. He's had a stroke.'

'So the uncle holds the cards?'

'Not quite all of them. The mother is the sister of one of the Khedive's wives.'

'God spare us harem politics!'

'My thought entirely. Mind you though, McPhee says the mother is very nice.'

Owen groaned.

'And he says the daughter is too.'

'Marie, this is?'

'Well, I'm not on Christian name terms with her – Owen, how comes it that you are? I thought you knew nothing about all this.'

'I do know nothing about all this. But as it happens, I have been approached by an interested party.'

'Exactly who? Come on, out with it, Gareth.'

'The sixth form at the Khedivial.'

There was a silence.

'The sixth form at the Khedivial? The Girls' Khedivial?'

'That's right.'

'Did you say you had been approached? By them?'

'That's right.'

'Gareth, your contacts are unrivalled and I am full of admiration.'

'Marie is in their class.'

'Marie, is it?'

'Yes. She's the one who has been kidnapped. The prime mover in all this appears to be Layla.'

'Layla. Yes, I see.'

'She's quite a girl, Paul.'

'I'm sure she is. Gareth, does Zeinab know about this?'

'I don't think so. In fact, I must tell her.'

'You certainly must.'

'In fact, they wanted to approach her themselves.'

'They?'

'The sixth form. The movers in all this.'

'Layla and that lot?'

'Yes. They wanted action, you see, and weren't getting it. Action over Marie, I mean, and they thought that if they worked on Zeinab, she would work on me.'

'I see, yes. So, actually, we're getting to the same place. Only in my case much later than everyone else. We all want you to take over the negotiations!'

'I'm not very keen myself.'

'Too bad, old boy. The weight of Egypt is against you.'

There was a long pause. Then, 'Gareth, I am reeling far behind in all this. But exactly why was it that they wanted to approach Zeinab? I yield to no one in my admiration for Zeinab, but . . .'

'Actually, I think you do. The senior girls at the Khedivial are all great admirers of Zeinab. They see her as a New Woman. New in Egypt, at any rate. A woman who stands up for herself, and other women generally, and gets things done. In the face of opposition from people like Marie's uncle. The old men who have had their day and are trying to block off Egypt from entry into the modern world. And especially blocking off women.'

'Suffragettes, that sort of thing?'

'That sort of thing, yes.'

'Well, good for them, say I. But I think they'll have a hard job in Egypt.'

'Impossible job, I agree, but good on them for trying.'

'They're the voice of the young, I suppose.'

'And we're the views of the old! It's the end of the dinosaurs, Paul, and we're among the dinosaurs!'

Nikos put his head around the door.

'Kewfik Efendi to see you,' he said.

'Kewfik?'

But it wasn't the uncle who came in but a much younger man.

'Hello, Owen,' he said confidently. He put out his hand. 'Ali Osman Fingari; I don't think we've met. I'm handling things now. For my father and, of course, for my uncle. At the Khedive's request. The fact is, Owen, my father's getting a bit doddery now and there's a mountain, an absolute mountain, of things for him to do, especially now that my uncle is *hors de combat* – did you know that he had had a stroke? Well, he has and my father has taken over. And he's asked me to help him out. Actually, it was the Khedive's idea. He said that my father is getting on a bit and we should be looking for ways of reducing the burden on him not adding to it. And perhaps taking over from my uncle in the negotiations over the girl – you know about that, of course? – is about the last straw, and maybe we should take the chance to look to the future.

'Well, you know, the Khedive's quite right. The Old Man's getting a bit erratic thcsc days. I've suggested I help him out but he's strangely unwilling to hand things over. You know these old blokes! Unwilling to let go. I've been suggesting that to him for some time but he won't have it. There's plenty of time, he says. Well, there isn't, not in his case. If he doesn't watch out he'll end up in hospital like my uncle. I think that came as a bit of a shock to him. A bit of a warning, you know. I said to him, "Look, Father, you can't go on like this or you'll pay the consequences." Well, as I say, I have been trying to tell him this for some time without getting anywhere, but I think my uncle's stroke may have been a bit of a lesson, and then the Khedive put his oar in.

'I'm a bit of a rowing man, Owen, did you know that? I used to row when I was at Harrow. You know Harrow, of course? Didn't go there yourself, by any chance? No? Well, I did. They insisted I take up sport of some kind, so I took up rowing. You can do it sitting down. Never regretted it. Thought I might take it up again here, on the Nile, you know, just whizz up and down. Thought I might get up a crew over here, you know, but never got round to it. Now I never shall, I suppose. With all the new responsibilities coming in on me. I won't havc thc time.'

'This business of the girl . . .' said Owen.

'Oh, that won't take long to sort out. My father's been making too much of it. It's just a question of money, I tell him. Offer the chaps cnough and they'll be eating out of your hand! In the end, it'll be less bother! But he doesn't see it like that. He doesn't like the thought of giving money away. "It's just a girl!" he said. "It's just money!" I said. We've got plenty and if they won't take it, we can keep it! We can't lose!'

'And you're in touch with the kidnappers, are you?'
'Oh, that's being handled by one of my uncle's men.'
'Is he up to it?'
'He'd better be! Or I'll have the hide off him!'
'But can you rely on people like that?'
'Why not?'
'In situations of this sort, you don't want things to go wrong.'
'Beat them hard enough and they won't go wrong!'
'I was thinking of the Khedive.'
'The Khedive?'
'What he might say if they go wrong.'
'They won't go wrong!'
'I am glad you feel so confident, Kewfik Effendi.'
'It is true that they are inexperienced men, working high above their station.'
'Just remember the Khedive will be following everything you do, Kewfik Effendi.'
'Following everything I do?'
'Well, of course! So if anything goes wrong, you may be blamed more easily. Remember, too, that although you may think you have the ear of the Khedive, there will be others who think that too.'
'Others?'
'I understand that the girl's mother is the sister of one of the Khedive's wives.'
'Oh her, yes. But I have never paid her much attention.'
'I suggest you do so now, Kewfik Effendi. You are in an exposed position. Exposed positions can be dangerous. I speak as a friend.'
'Yes, yes. Thank you, Mamur Zapt.'
'Remember, you can always count on me for help.'
'I will, Mamur Zapt. I will – and thank you very much!'
'Just take care, that's all.'
'Thank you. Yes, thank you, Mamur Zapt. These cursed harem politics!'

TWO

This time there were two of them in the yard: Layla, whom he knew, and a more diminutive uniformed figure, whom she was clutching by the collar. Nikos, clearly wondering if there were yet more of them to come, entered the room, frowning his disapproval.

'She is here again!' he said.

'Show her in!'

Layla came in holding a tiny, terrified figure.

'This is Minya,' she said.

'Hello, Minya!'

'*Bonjour, monsieur*,' she just managed.

'Minya has something to tell you,' Layla said.

Perhaps she had, but she was so terrified that she couldn't utter. Layla gave her a shake and then, when words didn't roll out of her, took over the narrative herself.

'Minya goes to school with Marie every morning. There is a servant but Marie doesn't like to bother with him so sends him away. But Minya stays with her because her parents have asked Marie to look after her. She was with her that morning.'

'That morning?'

'When Marie disappeared.'

'So she saw . . .?'

'She didn't see anything. She was probably still half asleep. How Marie puts up with her I don't know. But she was with her that morning. Taking her to school as usual. They usually go through the souk. Marie likes to go through the bazaars so that she can look at the fabrics and see what new ones have come in. Also she likes to try out the perfumes.

'That is what they did that morning. Minya says they spent a long time trying out the perfumes because Marie couldn't make up her mind. They were getting late and Minya was worried – Minya worries very easily – but Marie said that she wanted to try out a scent just one more time. They were almost at the school gates so Marie said she would go back by herself and went off. Minya hurried on in, pretty sure that by this time she would be late for roll call, and she didn't see Marie again.

'She forgot all about her but later in the afternoon she heard people talking and began to guess that something had gone wrong. Everyone was asking where Marie was and Minya didn't like to say anything because she thought that Marie might not want her to say anything because she ought not to have gone into the souk to try out the perfumes. So she kept quiet and then when it was clear that people were really worried about Marie and beginning to think that something serious had happened to her, she was too frightened to say anything and hid in a corner of the playground until going home time and by then it was too late.

'She probably wouldn't ever have told anyone but she has a cousin in one of the upper forms and this cousin knew that Minya usually went to school with Marie and asked her directly, and then she burst into tears and wouldn't stop. The cousin wanted her to go to the Headmistress but she wouldn't. She was too frightened. So the cousin came and told me, and I thought of going to the Head with her but then I thought: what good would that do? Marie was probably already dead by that time, so I decided to bring her straight to you.'

Minya was now crying steadily.

'I wanted to tell someone, I really did. But I thought they would blame me.'

'As they should,' said Layla.

'I kept meaning to but kept putting it off.'

'Worm,' said Layla pitilessly.

'And then it got harder and then I heard someone say that Marie was probably dead, and I couldn't bear it! I knew it was my fault. I wanted to die. I tried to die, but it just wouldn't come! I want to die!'

'Don't think you're going to get off that lightly,' said Layla.

Minya went on crying.

Nikos stuck his head in and quickly retreated. One thing he could not cope with was children crying.

'She's dead, and I've killed her!' sobbed Minya.

'Yes, she probably is, and you have,' said Layla fiercely.

Owen decided to take a hand.

'She may not be,' he said. 'In fact, it's unlikely that she is. They will be wanting to make some money out of her so they'll keep her alive.'

Minya was inconsolable.

'It's my fault!' she sobbed. 'I killed her. I just want to die! Please, let me die!'

'Then make it quick!' said Layla.

'No, you didn't,' said Owen. 'She's almost certainly alive and well. They'll be looking after her very carefully.'

Minya stopped crying.

'Do you think so?' she said. 'Do you really think so?'

'They won't want to kill the goose that lays the golden eggs,' said Layla.

'I'm sure my father will pay anything,' said Minya.

'No, he won't!' said Layla. 'Just shut up, will you?'

'Minya,' said Owen, 'do you think you could show me the shop where you were trying out the perfumes?'

Minya lifted her face hopefully.

'Yes!' she said. 'Yes, I could.'

The Scentmakers' Bazaar was actually not far from Owen's office in the Bab-el-Khalk, tucked just inside the Bab-es-Zuweyla, one of the old gates of the city. Here were the Tentmakers' Bazaar, the Silk Bazaar, the Tunis Bazaar and the Scentmakers' Bazaar. There were other bazaars, of course, but these were the ones that hit you as you went in by the gate. The Tunis Bazaar, which was roofed over against the sun, was by far the most picturesque, with its embroidered saddlebags and tasselled praying carpets. The main thing that set it apart, however, were its shoes: the bright yellow shoes of Tunis. Its sellers wore the shoes around their neck and strolled around dangling them invitingly.

Beside all this brightness, the Scentmakers's Bazaar came almost as a shock. Here each shop was little more than a cupboard where the owner sat on the counter with his feet up and large bulbous bottles peeping out from under his gown like giant eggs. Spread along the surface of the counter were stoppered ivory balls with cavities for the perfumes. As people passed, the shopkeeper would lean out from his counter, pull out a stopper and dab a sample of the contents on the sleeve of passers-by.

Layla brushed all aside.

'Cheap!' she declared disdainfully.

Minya shrank back.

'Not cheap,' protested the store holder indignantly. 'The very best! Otto of roses, jasmine, amber, bananas—'

'Bananas?' said Layla. 'Who wants to go around smelling of bananas?'

'Wear in the souk,' said the shopkeeper, unruffled, 'and all the men come running!'

'That'll be the day,' said Layla.

The shopkeeper caught at Owen's sleeve.

'You like amber? Put in coffee.'

'In coffee?' said Owen.

'Very good.'

'I don't think so, thanks.'

Minya was watching wide-eyed.

The shopkeeper reached behind him and pulled out a large jar of what looked like aniseed balls. He offered them to Minya.

'Sweetie?' he said. 'You like?'

Minya wavered.

'Tastes good,' said the shopkeeper. 'You try.'

Minya looked at Owen.

'Let me try first,' said Owen.

The shopkeeper held out the jar. Owen took one and put it into his mouth.

He nodded to Minya.

She took one with alacrity.

'See?' said the shopkeeper. 'She not die!'

Just along the counter was a stack of small ivory boxes.

The shopkeeper saw him looking at them.

'For English lady,' he said. 'To keep pills in. English ladies take lots of pills. Malaria, dysentery, headache. Phenacetin, quinine. But quinine tastes bitter.' He pulled a face. 'Keep pills in box, you smell the perfume, forget the taste!'

'Seems a good idea!' said Owen. He took up one of the boxes and smelled inside, then he put the box back.

'I don't think so,' he said.

As they went to move on, their path was blocked by a woman with a tambourine.

The shopkeeper waved her away.

'Gipsy!' he said contemptuously.

They moved on through the bazaar along the line of closed in boxes, each with a man sitting inside it like a great big spider.

'You're sure it was that one?' said Owen.

Minya nodded and sucked her aniseed ball.

Layla was disappointed that nothing more happened, but that afternoon a fat Greek with apparently nothing much to do wandered through the bazaar and came to a stop outside the shop. He spent a long time looking at the perfumed soap.

'Can I help?' said the shopkeeper.

'I'm looking for something for my wife,' said the Greek. 'A little present. She thinks I am neglecting her.'

'A nice soap would put that right.'

'I've given her that before. Too many times.'

'Ah! You need something different then. One of these little boxes perhaps?'

'They look very nice but what would you do with them?'

'Keep pills in them.'

'Pills?'

'Yes. Women are always taking pills.'

'Well, that's true. Headaches, for instance. At least, that's what she says. But I think she uses them as an excuse. No one gets headaches like my lady!'

'And not always at the most convenient times!' said the shopkeeper, laughing.

'You're dead right. She's got some pills, of course, but she keeps losing them.'

'Ah! Well, I've got something that will put that right. One of these little boxes. They're just right for keeping pills in and they're scented too. Your wife will like that.'

'That sounds like a good idea.'

'The scent will take her mind off the headaches.'

'Yes, yes. I hadn't thought of that.'

'I'll tell you another thing too,' said the shopkeeper with a wink, 'each box has a nice perfume in it. There are lots of different ones so you can find one she likes. You'll know what puts her in the mood.' He gave another wink. 'It'll help things along.'

'What an excellent idea!'

'It works every time!'

'It does?'

'It's the scent you see. It relaxes them. You've got a lot of choice. Try out a few until you find the right one.'

'I will!'

The Greek sniffed at the different boxes.

'You've got to keep them separate,' said the shopkeeper. 'That's why I put them in boxes.'

'I'll try three, for a start. I can always come back for more if they don't work.'

'It'll work all right. One of them.'

'But which one? That's the question, isn't it?'

'It is. But you can afford to experiment. They don't cost much.'

'I'll take these.'

'Fine. I'll wrap them up for you. You don't want her to see, do you? Keep it as a bit of a surprise.'

'I will, yes.'

The shopkeeper put them in a bag and then stopped.

'You said you were a bit tense?'

'Did I? Well, I am a bit occasionally, I suppose.'

'Try this one out for yourself. It's on the house. If you like it, you can come back.'

'It looks like paste.'

'It is paste. Sort of.'

'I expected it to be a liquid, like the others.'

'I can find you one in liquid form. But try the paste.'

'It doesn't smell much.'

'Oh, it will. When you get used to it. It will, and it will give you lovely dreams. You can smoke it. In fact, it's best if you do. It will ease the nerves very quickly.'

'It certainly would,' said Owen. 'It's pure opium!'

The Greek, who was one of Owen's agents, and whose name was Georgiades, licked his finger and touched the paste, then put his finger in his mouth.

'Strong!' he said. 'I hope he wasn't putting this among the aniseed balls.'

'No. I tested them before letting her have one. He keeps this for special customers.'

'Like schoolgirls?'

'I don't think so,' said Layla. 'She never talked about it, if she did. Of course, we've all tried it a bit. Hashish, usually, and only in very small doses, and among people you know. So that they could look after you if things went wrong. But no one, as far as I know, took it regularly. It's a thing you do when you go into the seniors, you know, to show you're big. But you only do it once or twice, and then you stop. You've got other things to do, but it is a phase you go through.'

'You yourself?'

'Once or twice. Once to see what it was like, and then again to see if it was always like that. I didn't like it much. It made my head spin, and I don't like my head doing that. I want to be, well, in control, I suppose. But other people did it more. There was a bit of a craze for it at one time, but then it sort of dropped away. It was at about that time that we became seriously interested in the New Woman. At first it was mostly a question of what you were wearing, outside school of course, of how you talked, that sort of thing, and, of course, we read magazines feverishly to know what we should be doing.'

'And that didn't include taking opium?'

'Oh, no. Cocaine, perhaps. But that's in Paris. Actually, I don't know much about Paris. It always seems very glamorous. We talk about it a lot. I would certainly like to go there but I don't expect to find the streets paved with hashish.'

'Clothes, mostly, that was what we're interested in. The great French fashion houses. The latest fashions. They're so different from what we have to put up with. School uniform! I don't think it's a good idea for a school to insist on uniform. It just makes people rebellious. I sometimes think that's why they keep uniforms, it's something innocuous to rebel against. To keep our minds off other things.

'The seniors are pretty divided on it. Some won't have the uniform at any price. Others, and I am one, say better the school uniform than the burka. Fortunately, our mothers tend to agree with us. Of course, dress is important in Egypt. For women, I mean. It's a sort of indication of where you stand. The hideous burka, for example. It makes you look as if you've come in straight from the country! And it hides you. It denies you. Suppose you were on the beach at Alexandria and tried wearing a burka!

'So what can you do? Wear Western, I suppose. Like your mother. The trouble is, mothers don't like that. Frightened of the competition, I suppose. So it's back to the burka, or school uniform. If I was going on the beach at Alexandria, I think I'd wear the uniform. It would be a bit of a gesture. But our fathers wouldn't like that. They don't want us going on the beach at all. Helene says wear uniform but just lift the hem a bit. The men would go crazy. But in a way that's the point of it.

'So there it is: even uniform is not safe. So instead we concentrate on the veil. That's what fashionable women in Cairo do anyway. "But it's just a veil," we say, when a dirty old man protests, "and you wouldn't want me to go out without a veil, would you?" Of course, it's a bit of a tease when you're a senior. You don't need a veil when you're a junior, because you're just a little girl. But when you're senior, it's a bit different. You'd be amazed at how much scope there is in the veil. Long, short, but the main thing is what it's made of. Does the material suggest rather than conceal? My mother spends hours trying to work that out. What does Zeinab do, Mamur Zapt? I bet you have never noticed. Well, most men do and *all* women certainly do. It is tricky when you get to the seniors. You don't want to go too far, but you certainly want to go as far as you can go. I would like to talk to Zeinab about this. Mothers are pretty useless when it comes to this sort of thing. You can't go out in something your mother was wearing ninety years ago!

'Marie? She goes for things which are pretty stylish. Her mother's not bad in that respect. Marie—'

She pulled her veil over her face and her shoulders began to shake. Sometimes the veil had its uses.

Minya's parents came to see Owen and said that something had to be done about her now that Marie had disappeared, indeed, had been kidnapped, for everyone now knew that Marie had been kidnapped. There was no chance of keeping something like that secret in a place like Cairo. At once parents begin to worry that their child might be next. In particular they worried that she might be seized on her way to school, as Marie had been. Extra policing was demanded.

There was, however, a more urgent need in Minya's case. Now that Marie had been abstracted from the scene, it was hoped temporarily, an escort was needed to take her place to and from school. Minya's father, who was a high-up in the Parquet, sought Owen's advice.

'Minya is too small to go on her own. Her mother wants you to assign a policeman to take her. I wouldn't quite go as far as that, but some senior girl perhaps? Of course, a policeman too.'

Owen had already been thinking along those lines. After a while, he had hit on Layla. She seemed a pretty capable girl, exuding responsibility, or so it seemed to Owen, at every pore. He consulted the Khedivial Headmistress.

'Oh, yes,' the Headmistress had said, 'she would do very nicely. She is a good, responsible girl. In fact, we have her in mind for our next Head Girl, and Minya likes her. She stands rather in awe of her, which is not a bad thing, girls being what they are.'

So Owen then asked Layla if she would be willing to take on this responsibility and Layla, who was one of those girls who never turned a responsibility down, had said that she would be willing.

'I suppose,' said Minya's father, 'that a policeman is hardly needed now.'

Owen had been thinking about this too. He did not, though, wish to be too ostentatious otherwise everyone would want one. He asked McPhee to give out that for a time there would be extra patrols, and then quietly went to have a word with one of the likely patrollers. This was Selim, a giant Nubian, who would certainly be a match for any five or six ordinary kidnappers, and whom he had worked with before.

He summoned Selim.

'You see this little girl? I want you to take her to school in the morning and then pick her up after school in the afternoon and see she gets home safely. You will be assigned to patrols in the area, which you should carry out for the rest of the day, so

that everyone will get used to seeing you about. That will reassure
people. I want you, though, to keep a particular eye on that little
girl as someone has kidnapped the friend she goes to school with
and she may still be rather shaken.'

'Effendi, I will keep two eyes open and if I see a kidnapper
I will knock his block off.'

'That will do nicely.'

Selim was introduced to Minya.

'Why,' said Selim, 'it is a little pigeon! Hello, little pigeon,
just come with me and you'll be all right.'

'There is a lot of you,' said Minya critically.

'All the better to look after you with,' said Selim. He had no
children of his own, and this was a great disappointment to him
and his wife. They still lived in hope, but the years were going
by. Fatima, his wife, who was nearly as large as Selim, came
out and inspected Minya.

'Keep him in order for me,' she said to Minya. 'He is all right
if you tell him what to do.'

'I will,' Minya promised gravely, and they went off hand in
hand.

Owen was going out that night with an Egyptian friend of his,
Mahmoud el Zaki. Mahmoud was in the Parquet, the Department
of Prosecutions of the Ministry of Justice. The Egyptian legal
system was not like the English. It was based more on the French
system. When a crime was reported in Egypt it was at once taken
over not by the police but by the Parquet, who then took the case
and saw it through to prosecution in court. The Parquet was full
of bright young Egyptians intensely ambitious not just for a
successful legal career but usually also for a political one. They
were, therefore, continually at loggerheads with the British administration, which liked to keep the governance of the country to
itself. Owen and Mahmoud disagreed violently about this,
Mahmoud tending to the view that governing Egypt was a thing
for Egyptians and not for the British. Nevertheless, politics aside,
the two of them got on very well. And their concord had recently
been reinforced by Mahmoud's wife, Aisha, having a third baby.
Till now, Owen and Zeinab had none. It was too complicated,
they felt. He was British and she was Egyptian; he was a senior

member of the British Administration and she the daughter of a Pasha still active in politics. Nevertheless, a baby had thrust itself on to the international stage, albeit at a humble level, and both Mahmoud and Aisha were killing themselves with laughter at the way in which their friends' lives had been turned upside down.

Aisha and Mahmoud had not yet seen the new baby and, as babies were more readily transportable than three small children, they were on this occasion the hosts. They went outside at once into Mahmoud's small garden, beneath the orange trees and banana trees. Egyptian gardens were built for shade rather than flowers.

The meal was a mixture of Egyptian and English, although mostly Egyptian: peanut soup, which Aisha knew Owen particularly liked, stuffed aubergines, roast pigeons, a salad of tomatoes, onions and nasturtium flowers, and finally apricots and rice pudding. They drank iced lemonade rather than wine, since Mahmoud and Aisha were both Muslim, and then there was Turkish coffee.

After that they all went to review the babies.

After agreeing that the babies were each as lovely as the other, Owen and Mahmoud went outside as there was something they particularly wanted to discuss.

'This Kewfik girl,' said Mahmoud, 'you know about her?'

'The one who has been kidnapped?'

'That's the one.' He looked at Owen curiously. 'How do you come to know about her? They have been trying to keep it quiet, while negotiations are proceeding.'

'Not much hope of that. But, in answer to your question, I was approached and asked about it. I was approached by a friend of the Kewfik girl. Apparently her friends in the Khedivial had been putting two and two together and not getting, in their view, very satisfactory answers. Not from the school, nor from the police, nor from the family.'

'The father has had a stroke and is in hospital.'

'And an uncle is handling it. Not very skilfully.'

'He wouldn't be able to handle a cup of coffee skilfully.'

'It has been officially reported, I take it? No? Then how?'

'The girl's mother is the sister of one of the Khedive's wives.

So the back stairs have been positively humming. Especially as they don't care for the uncle much. They don't think he is up to the job.'

'Of negotiating with the kidnappers? That is my information too.'

'And your information comes from . . .?'

'The senior girls at the Khedivial. Marie's friends.'

'I don't think they ought to be getting themselves mixed up in this.'

'Nor do I, really, but they've mixed themselves up in it and . . .'

'And?'

'They're hard to stop. One of them has been to see me. She went to see McPhee and the police threw her out.'

'They ought not to have done that.'

'So she came to see me. As second best.'

'After McPhee?'

'After Zeinab.'

'Zeinab!'

'They thought they were more likely to get a sensible response out of a woman.'

'Well, yes – but . . .'

'The senior girls at the Khedivial are not like the girls you and I used to know. They are more liberated. Modern. And they think that things are stacked against women in Egypt, and even more stacked against young girls like Marie. And, you know, if people like the uncle are handling things, they could be right.'

'They could, but . . .'

In Egypt at that time such things were always handled by men.

'Is there not some other man who could oversee the negotiations?' said Mahmoud.

'My thoughts exactly.'

'And theirs, too, it appears.'

'Theirs?'

'The wives. The harem wives, the Khedive's wife's sister and all that.'

'The back stairs?'

'And, of course, the front stairs. If you think of yourself as front.'

'The Khedivial girls, you mean?'

'I do. Who seem to me to be learning as fast as their mothers. Anyway, the upshot is that the Khedive himself is taking a hand. The wives have persuaded him to put the whole thing in the hands of someone more sensible than the uncle.'

'Well, that's a relief.'

'It is,' said Mahmoud. 'And conversely, it is not.'

'I'm sorry?'

'You're not going to like this. The person into whose hands he is putting it is you.'

'Me?'

'The Khedive's Chief of Intelligence, the right-hand man. The Mamur Zapt. Which will show everyone how seriously he is taking it. This is at the special request of the harem wives. Which shows who really has the power around here.'

'I – I really don't think . . .'

'Nor does the Parquet. They think they should be handling it. So does the Cabinet, and the Pashas. In fact, nobody thinks that you should be handling this. Except the Khedive and the harem wives, of course. And police, I should add to the list; and the senior girls at the Khedivial. A formidable alliance, Gareth. You don't stand a chance!'

Zeinab and Aisha came into the room carrying the new babies.

'Have you heard the news?' said Aisha brightly. 'At last they're doing something about that poor Kewfik girl. Only don't tell anyone. It's top secret!'

THREE

The next morning Mahmoud was working in the Geziret, a poor area just the other side of the Gare Centrale, one of Cairo's main stations. He knew the area quite well. About a year before he had been there when a little boy had been knocked over by an arabeah, one of Cairo's horse-drawn carriages. The arabeah had been taking a passenger to the station and would not have stopped, but Mahmoud had stepped in its way and compelled it to. A three-way altercation had ensued – the driver, the passenger and Mahmoud. Mahmoud had suggested that the arabeah at least pick the boy up, but the arabeah had been rushing to catch a train. To save argument the passenger, a rich man, possibly a Pasha, had thrown the boy a handful of milliemes and hurried on. Mahmoud had gone with the child to his house which lay just beyond the tracks. The grateful family had offered Mahmoud a cup of tea and while he was drinking it the father had mentioned that he worked for the Kewfik family, who owned a large complex of stables nearby.

They had been sitting on the ground in front of the house and a small crowd had gathered, as was usual in Egypt when anything interesting like an accident happened. Among the crowd were some rough-looking individuals who had sidled up in rather a threatening way. Parquet officers were not unused to such situations and Mahmoud knew how to handle it. However, action on his part proved to be unnecessary, for the father of the boy stood up in a fury and drove the men off.

Afterwards, over a further cup of tea which the family had insisted upon, the father had said that lately there were too many bad people hanging around and that he found them near all the big houses. The Kewfik drivers were always having to chase them away. It was then that he mentioned that he himself was a stableman at the Kewfiks. He said that it had not always been like this but had got worse lately. Mahmoud had wondered why this should be. The father didn't know but thought it might be to do with politics, which was the universal explanation in Egypt for trouble.

Mahmoud had stored the story away in his mind, in a policeman-y sort of way. He thought no more of it at the time. Now, however, the attention to the Kewfiks rang a bell and he was turning the episode over in his mind as he went past the stables, when he was hailed by a woman. It was the mother of the boy he had picked up. He greeted her back and asked how the boy was doing. Well, God be praised, and no thanks to that arabeah driver. Her husband had asked around at the stables when he got back but it had not been one of their men. That made it doubly bad, for what was an interloper doing in their district?

He asked after her husband. Well, she said, at the stables there was always dung to clear.

'And do the bad men still hang around?' Mahmoud asked.

'It's got worse,' she said. 'It's got worse since that girl went missing. For now the police are here every day asking questions.'

'So they should be,' said Mahmoud, 'when a child goes missing.'

'She is more than a child,' the woman said. 'It is getting to the time to marry her off.'

'And would she like that?' asked Mahmoud.

'What girl would not?' asked the woman.

'I speak from ignorance,' said Mahmoud. 'My own are too small.'

'How many?' asked the woman, interested.

'Three at the moment.'

'You're young still. Soon there will be more and then there will be too many!' She laughed.

'A while yet,' said Mahmoud. He felt rather shy about talking of such things with a comparative stranger. 'How many do you have?' he asked.

'Five,' said the woman. 'But we have lost two.'

'A blow,' said Mahmoud.

She shrugged.

'But also a relief,' she said.

She said that she had often seen Marie setting out for school. Along with a little one.

'That is good to see,' she said. 'Daughters should learn to care for little ones. Although it is surprising that they would walk and

not take an arabeah. It's not like the Kewfiks can't afford it.
Although they do say that the older girl likes to go through the
souk. Well, you can understand that. There's much to see.'

'And smell,' said Mahmoud.

'And smell. They always went through the Scentmakers, so
people say. Well, you can understand that too. Girls always like
a bit of scent and they like it more the older they get!'

Mahmoud laughed.

'I have yet to find that out,' he said.

She laughed too.

'You will,' she said. 'You will! It won't be long before your
girls have their admirers!'

'Did the Kewfiks' girl have an admirer?' he asked.

'Oh yes! Several. They used to wait for her in the afternoon
when she came out of school. But she just laughed and sent them
packing.'

'I don't know how they find the time,' Mahmoud said. 'I had
to go home to my books the moment I left school in the afternoon
or my father would be on to me.'

'Ah, he was a proper father!'

'As a matter of fact,' said Mahmoud, 'as much as I respected
him, there were times when I rather regretted that.'

'I bet there were,' said the woman, giggling.

Mahmoud, always awkward when it came to chatting with
women, thought it was time to steer the conversation back away
from himself.

'Had she reached the stage of favouring any particular boy?'
he asked.

'There was a time when we thought so, about a year ago.
There was a boy who used to follow her round like a pet Passover
lamb. He even bought her scent! She laughed and said it would
be no good putting that on because her mother would know in
a flash that she'd been out with a boy! She made him take it
back. They were very close for a while but it came to nothing.'

'Do you remember the boy's name?'

'Ridwan, was it? Ibrahim? No, Ali. Ali Shawquat, one of the
Shawquat boys. The quietest of them. I always remember him
because he played the *nay*!'

'The *nay*?'

'All the time. He used to go to the stables when Ibrahim was working there and sit there, as good as gold, just playing his *nay*. Of course, his father didn't like it. I mean, playing it a bit is one thing, but playing it all the time is another. They say that was one of the things that made him send the boy away. Others say that it wasn't that, it was that the Kewfiks didn't like the way things seemed to be going between him and their girl. But my man, Ibrahim, says that it was because of the stone throwing.'

'Stone throwing?'

'In the bazaar a couple of days ago. You must have heard about it! Everyone was talking about it.'

The Greek put his head in at the perfume seller's.

'I thought I would just let you know that last night it worked like a treat!'

'It did? I'm glad.'

And a little surprised. However, he knew that a lot of these things were in the mind's eye.

'There may be the occasional night when it doesn't work,' he cautioned, 'but don't let that put you off. The next night you'll find that it's working again.'

'Oh, good.' Georgiades hesitated. 'Do you find that there are any side effects?'

'Side effects? Such as?'

'Well, fatigue. It could happen, you know. If you take it every night.'

'In that case, give thanks to God, and go on taking.'

The Greek still hesitated.

'I was thinking about the more general effects,' he said.

'Such as?'

'Well, if it has this effect on one family, what is it doing overall? I mean, if a lot of people are taking it?'

'Bully for them, I say!'

'Yes, but, suppose everyone started taking it?'

'There would be a lot of happy people around.'

'Yes, I know, but what would be the effects?'

'Universal happiness.'

'Look, you couldn't make *everyone* happy. It stands to reason and then some people are going to feel left out. Won't they complain?'

'Some people are just old miseries!'

The Greek was silent for a moment and then he started again.

'Isn't there going to be an effect on the population? I mean, won't everyone start having babies?'

'Well, of course, God is great.'

'True, true. But I was just thinking – I mean, Cairo is pretty crowded already.'

'Look, I am just a shopkeeper in the Scentmakers' Bazaar. I can't solve all the problems of the world! And nor can you. You worry too much, my friend!'

'People do say that.'

'Let others share the burden! And, look, if it's really getting you down, I've got something which might help.'

He took down a large bottle from behind him on the shelf.

'Take a couple of pills. It's on the house.'

'Really? You're sure? Well, thank you.'

'You can always come back for some more.'

The Greek took the pills and asked for some more of 'the paste sort'.

'Are you sure? I mean, you don't want to overdo it!'

'Actually, it's my wife.'

'She's asking for them? Well, you are in luck!'

'I don't know whether I ought to give them to her. I mean, suppose I get tired and she still wants to go on?'

'Give thanks to God!'

'But if I find I can't go on, and she still wants to, she may, you know, turn to other men.'

'Well, there is that problem, yes. Perhaps you'd better not let her have them!'

'Maybe one, just occasionally.'

'That sounds sensible. You know, my friend, you are a bit of a worrier. Just relax a bit!'

'I keep thinking: suppose everyone took those pills, and everyone has a baby. The streets would be full of them. You wouldn't be able to walk along! And what about the camels?'

'Camels?'

'And donkeys. They wouldn't be able to get around. Not with all the babies in the way.'

'I really wouldn't bother too much about that!'

The Greek smiled.

'I worry too much, you think? Well, I probably do. Can't solve all the world's problems, that right?'

'You take too much on yourself.'

'I probably do.'

He picked up the pills.

'Oh, by the way – do you know a Mother Shawquat? She lives somewhere around here.'

'I know the Shawquat family. Who doesn't?'

'It's like that, is it?'

'That boy of theirs! Rampaging through the souk! We're just ordinary shopkeepers, you know, finding it hard to make ends meet and what we don't need is a bunch of hooligans going through the place, upsetting stalls, tipping things out, spoiling what we've got to sell, throwing stones . . .'

'Throwing stones! That's terrible!'

'What have we done to deserve that? We're only little people. Poor people. These hoodlums forget that or maybe they don't care!'

'Actually throw stones?'

'Yes! Here, I'll show you.'

He got down off the counter and went to the back of the stall. He put his hand up and pointed to some splintering on the woodwork.

'There! And it's like that everywhere in this part of the souk. Things ruined. People hit! Look there!'

He pointed to a mark on his cheek.

'They didn't do that!'

'They did! And worse. A man just up the row had his head cut open. Right open. Bleeding. Blood everywhere! Why did they have to do that? Might have knocked his eye out. Might have knocked *my* eye out!'

'And this was a bunch of . . .?'

'Hooligans! Students. Just breaking up the place.'

'But why?'

'Protesting! They said they wanted to make a point.'

'But what sort of point do they think they're making by throwing stones?'

'You tell me!'

'There must be a reason. They must have done it for some reason.'

'It was against the Khedive and the British.'

'The British, I can understand, but the Khedive! That's just disloyal.'

'It's not that we're that much in favour of the Khedive. What's he ever done for us? Throw stones against the Khedive if you want to, but why throw stones at me? It's not right.'

'It's not! It's outrageous! Was there some reason? Some particular things that they didn't like?'

'It's because we just sat there, they said. Instead of getting up and throwing stones like them.'

'That's unreasonable!'

'That's students for you!'

'Ah, they were students, were they?'

'So they said. But I'll bet they've never opened a book in their lives!'

'And – and this boy Shawquat?'

'He was the ringleader. Several of us recognised him. They went through the souk just like that, breaking up everything. Turning tables over. Wrecking stalls.'

'Not your stall?'

'Yes! My stall too. Luckily I saw it coming and put the best jars under the counter. All the same, they broke some. The place was smelling like the Khedive's harem afterwards.'

'And this boy, Shawquat, the ringleader, you say – what does he have against the Khedive?'

'The whole gang of them, they think he's too close to the British. It's to teach him a lesson.'

'They're the ones who need to be taught a lesson. And I reckon they will be too, when the British get around to them.'

'The British don't care. Not about the Khedive. Not about the likes of us!'

'Yes, but, I mean the souk! You cannot just let people go smashing up the souk.'

'That's what I said! Where will it stop, I said.'

'You reported it, of course?'

'Of course! And a fat lot of good that did. The thing was, though, that they upset a barrow belonging to one of the Kauris and that was a mistake. The Kauris are a big family and a rough lot and they pitched into them and sent them packing and that was the end of it. It was nothing to do with the police or the Khedive or the British. It was that they'd crossed the Kauris.'

'And they chased the hooligans off? The students?'

'That's right. It's one thing coming in here and turning over a few tables. It's another dealing with the Kauris.'

'And this boy Shawquat?'

'Got out pretty fast. Having started all the trouble.'

'Maybe that was the idea?' suggested the Greek mildly.

Minya, playing in a corner of the playground, came across a large pebble. It was smooth and round and had pretty red markings on it. She picked it up and went to show it to her cousin, who was in the form above.

'You want to throw that away,' said the cousin, 'or else they'll start blaming you!'

'What for?' said Minya, worried.

'Throwing it at people. That is what they were doing in the souk the other day.'

Minya dropped it like a hot potato.

She was still worrying about it when school came out at the end of the afternoon, and after much thought found it again and took it out to Selim, who she knew would be waiting for her outside the gates.

'I don't know what to do with it,' she said.

Selim looked at it.

'It's just a stone,' he said.

'No,' said Minya, 'it's a special stone.'

'How's that then?' said Selim, taking the stone and slipping it into a fold of his galabiya.

'They were throwing it the other day in the souk. All the girls were talking about it. Our Head teacher kept us in until they had stopped.'

'That was very sensible of her,' said Selim.

'You ought not to throw stones at people,' said Minya.
'Someone might have got hurt.'

'They might. Don't you go round throwing stones, little pigeon.'

'No, I won't,' promised Minya. 'Marie's friend was one of the
boys throwing stones and she was cross with him.'

'Oh, yes?' said Selim vaguely. He was aware of the throwing
stones episode, everyone in the souk was, but, like him, vaguely.

Minya looked up sharply.

'You know about Marie. She's the one who used to walk me
to school before you did and now Layla, and one day she was
kidnapped, and it was all my fault!'

'What?' said Selim, waking up suddenly.

'Some bad men. They kidnapped her, and it was all my fault!'
She began to cry.

'Now, now!' said Selim, not used to children's tears, and much
agitated. 'What's all this?'

'They took her away and might have killed her, and Layla
says it was all my fault!'

'No, no, they won't. You've got it wrong, little pigeon, it's not
your fault. But what does this have to do with the stone?'

'Marie. She walked me to—'

'The Kewfik girl is this?'

Despite the efforts to keep quiet about the kidnapping word
had not only got out but was all round the souk.

Minya burst into more tears.

Selim paused, still holding Minya. Lacking children of his
own, he didn't quite know what to do with her.

He decided to take her back to the Bab-el-Khalk. The boss
would know.

Owen was not in fact in his room, but Georgiades, alerted by
the sound unusual in the Bab-el-Khalk of a child crying, and
having children of his own, came out of a door further along the
corridor. Selim seemed incapable of explaining how he came to
be in the police headquarters with a distressed child in his arms.

Minya fumbled in the pockets of his galabiya and produced
the stone.

Georgiades examined it gravely.

'It looks a good stone,' he said. 'How does it come to be
there?'

Selim's mouth opened and closed wordlessly.

'I picked it up in the playground,' said Minya, 'and my cousin said it looked like one of the stones the boys had been throwing, and that I ought to throw it away, or else the police would be on to me.'

'No, we wouldn't,' said Georgiades, 'not unless there was some reason to think you had been throwing it.'

'Marie was cross with her boy friend because he had been throwing it.'

'This one?'

'Or one like it. He had been throwing them in the souk. That day when everyone was doing it.'

Feeling important, Minya sat on the end of the desk in the fat man's room. He sat on a chair opposite her and seemed harmless. He spoke to her in the same way as the Mamur Zapt had done, as equal to equal. Layla had said that was what she liked about him. Men, she said, usually give themselves airs. If they could be bothered to notice the presence of a girl – or young woman rather. Minya knew that she shouldn't say girl, she was a young woman and should not forget it, said Layla. Although on the whole Minya felt more like a little girl than she did a grown up.

The Mamur Zapt, however, was approved of by Layla and the other big girls and Minya knew better than to buck the trend. Besides, she quite liked the Mamur Zapt, although he was rather tall and she did not really understand all this about a Zeinab or where she fit in. Who was she? Perhaps she was the Mamur Zapt's mother. But if so, why did he not just call her mother? Most children Minya knew were not on first name terms with their parents. But Minya was finding that there were a lot of things she did not know and that this was probably another.

The fat man was quite nice and not at all intimidating (this was a word she had recently learned and was rather proud of).

The fat man put his hand in his pocket and took out an object, then placed two things on the desk, both of which Minya recognised. The first was the stone and the second was a sweet. She had seen that before too, in the Scentmakers' Bazaar.

'So here is my question,' said the fat man: 'do they both come from the same place?'

Minya thought they did. Perhaps they were not exactly the same, but they were very like the stones that had been thrown in the Bazaar and the sweets that had been in the jar – on the scentmaker's counter.

'Your friend Marie would probably recognise them too,' said the fat man.

Minya nodded.

'Did the man in the shop give her sweets?' asked Georgiades.

'Sometimes.'

'But I'll bet she didn't throw stones!' said the fat man.

Minya was quite sure of this.

'In fact, she told off her friend when he threw them?'

Minya nodded again.

'Who was this friend?'

'Marie's friend. I don't know his name,' said Minya firmly.

'Did she meet him often?'

Minya considered.

'Quite often,' she said.

'When she was taking you to school? Or when you were coming home?'

'Both. But not always in the afternoon because he had lectures.'

Minya thought she needed to explain.

'Lectures are like lessons,' she said.

'And then one day they started throwing stones? Like this one?'

'Yes,' said Minya. 'And one of them nearly hit me, and I didn't like it and Marie became very angry and said, "What the hell did they think they were doing?"' She remembered the word exactly because it was one that children were told not to use, and she had been quite shocked when she heard Marie using it. Although a little thrilled.

Marie had pulled her behind one of the wooden booths. But then the boys had started breaking up the booth. And Marie had come out and shouted at them, and they had run away. Then one of the boys had said to Marie's friend: 'Who the hell's side do you think you're on?'

'Hell' again. It had marked it firmly in Minya's mind. The boy and Marie's friend had started shouting at each other and Minya had been afraid they were actually going to hit each other, but the other boys pulled them apart and told them to get on with it. And they had all moved off to another part of the souk and Marie had been of half a mind to go with them, but then she remembered Minya and stopped.

'You're a little pain in the ass!' she had said to Minya and Minya had started crying but Marie had grabbed her and hugged her and said it was all right, it wasn't her fault. But Minya had known that she wanted to go after the boys and had felt guilty once again.

'And what had happened then?' asked the Greek. It had all quietened down, and then someone had come running along the line of wrecked shops shouting to everyone to get out because the Kauris were coming. And Marie had grabbed her by the arm and pulled her away, and they had run out of the souk and off home.

'This was in the afternoon, was it?' asked the fat man. 'At the end of school, when you were on your way home?'

Minya agreed that it was.

'And all the shopkeepers were very cross,' she said.

Such incidents were not uncommon in Cairo. In fact, they happened all the time and the police were inclined to disregard them. It was irritating for the shopkeepers but, as McPhee said, it could have been much worse. Nationalism was stirring in Egypt and the student body was generally restive. It was part, thought Owen, of growing up in a society that was just becoming conscious of the possibilities that were opening up for it. Handle with care, was Owen's motto. Because if you didn't handle it with care a situation would explode – and there was already the possibility of explosion. But so long as it remained only a possible explosion and did not become an actual explosion, you were all right. He judged that this incident was already settling back to the possible level and not worth worrying too much about.

But there was one thing that stood out: the involvement of Marie Kewfik's friend. How deep did that involvement go? And was there any connection between it and Marie Kewfik's kidnapping?

FOUR

When Mahmoud had worked in the Geziret previously he had had occasion to visit several of the schools in the area. Among them was the school that Ali Shawquat had attended – it was in the same area dominated by the Kewfik stables and most of the bigger children who still went to school in that area went there. Mahmoud had liked the school and liked the Headmaster. He was a decent man, a little unimaginative, perhaps, but one who knew his children. Mahmoud decided to pay him a visit.

Yes, the Headmaster remembered Ali Shawquat: a promising boy, of whom they had had great hopes. He had been a prefect and looked on as a possible future Head Boy. Egyptian schools were usually modelled on the English system and went in for such things as Head Boys. Mahmoud himself had been Head Boy. But this school was very different from the one he had attended. Mahmoud had gone to a school for the very brightest children. It was for the sons of the Cairo elite and was much like a good English grammar school. The school young Shawquat had attended had been more like a technical school, but a good one which tended to do well by its boys. Its aim was to open doors for humbler children of ability and, with its sympathetic and committed Headmaster, to give its pupils a good start in life; for the area, that was. He had gone on from the school to a senior technical college, where he had studied engineering. This was the best route for the bright boy from the Geziret. Brighter boys went to one of the religious foundations. The most famous of these was, of course, the El Azhar. However, his grades at school had not been good enough for him to go there, nor did his inclination.

'His interests were elsewhere?'

'I don't think his interests were clearly defined when he was still with us, but they were certainly not in a religious direction.' This in a way was significant. Egypt was a Muslim country and most bright students went into religious study. You had to make a conscious effort not to.

'In his case what helped was parental influence,' went on the Headmaster. 'Usually it is the father but in Shawquat's case it was the mother as well. He had an unusually strong-minded mother who wanted him to be equipped for life in the modern world. It was a good thing, I think. I do not say this because I am not a good Muslim. God forbid! But it doesn't suit everyone and I don't think it would have suited him. His was a peasant family and not at all inclined to religious speculation. But, unlike a lot of peasant families, they were ambitious for their son. The mother especially. "My boy is not going to work in the fields!" she told me more than once. "He is a clever boy and deserves better."

'And the father, too, was ambitious for his son. Back then, at least, he was a strong radical which meant that he was not content with his place and he thought that society was holding him back, keeping him down. So he was angry with society – bitter against it, bitter against the Pashas, bitter against the Khedive. Bitter against the Kewfiks, who are the big employers around here.'

'Bitter against the Kewfiks?'

'Yes. Why do you sound surprised? Everyone here is bitter against the Kewfiks. Especially those who work for them. As Ali Shawquat's father did, in the stables. The Kewfiks own the land. Their overseer's whip lands across the peasants' backs. Perhaps I shouldn't say that, but that is how it seems to the peasants. They know only what it meant for them.'

'So young Ali grew up with a mother who wanted better things and a father who knew only that he was against the bosses, and both mother and father pinned their hopes on him,' Mahmoud said, nodding his head.

'Yes, but he wasn't really like what either of them wanted. He was a mild, brainy boy who loved music. He used to play the *nay* very well and we encouraged him. It seemed to lift him and, as time went by, it began to seem that he wasn't suited to anything else. He was not really interested in his technical studies, in the technical school. He was always cutting away to play by himself. In fact, his mother paid for him to have music lessons, but this was not what his father wanted at all. His father saw him as a boss in some factory or other, making a lot of money. But Ali did not want to be a boss, he did not want to work in a factory. So there was trouble between them.

'The parents came to me and said: "What shall we do? All he is interested in is the *nay*, but playing the *nay* will not bring us money to keep a family or build a house – or provide for us when we are old."

'I put this to him and he said that his life was the *nay*. He didn't want to do anything else. His father struck him and bullied him and said that what he wanted to do was do nothing but how could a family afford that?'

'That would have been difficult for the boy.'

'And there was another consideration: both his mother and his father were ardent nationalists. His father was a member of the Nationalist Party. They were working, they said, for a better Egypt, an Egypt in which wrong was righted and life would be better for everyone. What was wrong with him, that he couldn't do that?

'The mother said: "Why did he think only of himself?" and his father said: "On my money! Let him provide for himself if all he wants to do is play the *nay*?"

'They wanted me to appeal to him, and I did. I reasoned with him and said he had to think of his family, of others too. Of Egypt. Did he not want to help to build a better land? Like his father and mother?

'He said he did but he wanted to play the *nay* too.

'"Play the *nay*, by all means," I said, "but do it as well as providing for yourself and your family!"

'Well, I think he did heed what I said, and for a time there was an improvement in his work at the technical college. He was a clever boy and there could be no doubt about his ability to do well if he tried, but after a while he didn't try as much. He began to drift back to his *nay*. What didn't help was his fellow students. They kept saying, "Let us hear more of the *nay*! Factories go on forever but playing such as yours does not."'

'And his father did not like that?'

'His father had always disliked his *nay*-playing but he was cunning. When Ali's work began to fall off he did not blame the *nay*-playing, he blamed the work! It was not his fault, he said, the poor and lowly always have to struggle. It was society's fault, not his.

'"Look at the Kewfiks," he said. "Do they have to struggle? Don't you work as hard as they do? And yet they get further. Is that just?"

'Well, after a while he began to believe his father and then he began to work even less hard, and his performance at school fell off even more. He felt that it wasn't his fault and became bitter, and he added his father's bitterness to his own.

'He fell in with other discontented boys, unsuccessful students. They went round together and started to become a nuisance and we were sad, because we had seen it before. Bright children become less bright and in the end falling foul of the law. There were little bits of indiscipline, then larger. Stones were thrown. They made trouble in the souk. I have seen it before. One or two troublemakers join together and become so many troublemakers that the police take notice.

'That's how it was with the bunch that Ali had fallen in with. It soon became clear that the police would step in, and then what would happen to Ali? He would be punished, become known as a bad lot. It would be the end of all their bright hopes for their son.

'And then, just at this time, there began this business with the girl.'

'Marie Kewfik?'

'Yes. No sooner than I saw them together my heart began to sink, for the Kewfiks are a rich, powerful family and they would not like it. What seems like innocent play soon became less innocent. They grow up, and Ali began to grow up and she, too, I expect. At first it was just *nay* playing. When he played at the stables for the workmen, or after school in the playground for his fellow students, she would be there. There were others too, of course, lots; but she – she seemed riveted to him and the music. Soon she was always there, and it began to be noticed. The Kewfiks heard of it and someone must have spoken to Ali's father, for he intervened.

'"Rich are rich and poor are poor," he said to Ali, '"and they do not mix. Keep away from the girl!"

'Perhaps something similar was said on the Kewfiks' side,

because for a while we didn't see the two together. But then she began to come again, not in the stables, they stopped that, but after school to where Ali played daily in the playground.

'And all this time, his playing was getting better and better. The playground began to be full after school. Even the masters, even people nothing to do with the school, came to listen. And she was rapt.

'When he had finished for the day and went home, they went off together. Not to his home, nor to hers, but somewhere together. Always together.'

'Ali's father became angry?'

'Yes, very. "You will bring trouble upon us!" he said, and beat the boy. After a while Ali ran away. We don't know what happened to him, but we knew that he was still playing, and we suspected that she still went to listen.

'And then we heard one day that she too had gone. Kidnapped, some said. Run away like him, others said. But someone told us that she had been taken by someone else, bad men, who had seized her for money. Ali was walking around like a man who had lost his senses. And then, suddenly we no longer saw him about. And some said he had killed himself. Out of despair.'

'And what do you think?'

'We no longer hear his *nay*.' The Head looked thoughtful. 'There are police everywhere, but they are not looking for him. A poor man counts for nothing, but everyone looks for her.'

'What,' said Owen to Mahmoud, 'is a *nay*?'

'It is,' said Mahmoud, 'a kind of flute. It is, possibly, the most played instrument in Egypt. Children play it. Snake charmers play it. Itinerant beggars play it. Everyone plays it. It is where you start if you want to learn how to play music.'

'It must be fairly simple to play,' Owen suggested mildly.

'Oh, yes, and cheap too. It is really just a reed with holes in it. You blow through a tiny aperture with your lips pressed against the edge of the tube,' Mahmoud demonstrated using the side of a pencil, 'and the sound comes out through the holes. There are six holes in front and behind. By blowing with more or less force sounds are produced which can vary in pitch, some high, others low. A good performer can regulate the sound very precisely, and can even scale many octaves. A very good performer can produce lovely mellow tones. But only a very good performer. Someone who is good is worth going a long way to hear.'

'It sounds as if this Ali is like that.'

'We'll take you along to hear a good *nay* player some time.'

He went to see Layla and asked her about Marie's friends.

'Oh, she has lots!'

But, at that time, she went off by herself. She had done a lot of reading. Novels, certainly, mostly French ones because they had ideas in them and Marie was interested in ideas. But lately she had stopped that and seemed to want to talk. But there was no one she could talk to.

Surely, the other girls . . .

They were all right in their way but Marie wanted something different.

'Boy friends?'

Layla backed off a little at this. But then she recovered stoutly. Boy friends, certainly. But the boys of their age were not, in practice, intellectually of their age. They were a bit backward, really, that was the truth of it. And, anyway, their families went mad the moment they saw them with a boy! They hustled you away and your mother insisted on having a 'good talk' with you. As if you have never heard of love-making! And, indeed, a lot of the boys hadn't. No, said Layla, you could keep boys as far as she was concerned, and she thought Marie had felt the same way. But then she had started being interested in music.

Had Marie had a boy friend?

Well, she had and she hadn't. She had tried several boys out, boys who had been in the Khedivial Boys' School across the way, but found them wanting: too young, actually. So then she had tried out some of the boys from the colleges but found them unsatisfactory too: too old! They had wanted to push things along a bit further than she was comfortable with. And that was always the problem. Men had no sense of balance! They always wanted to go too far or too fast, or they didn't know what it was all about at all! Layla thought there was a big sex problem developing in Egypt. Boys couldn't talk to girls and girls couldn't talk to boys, not while they were the way they were. It was getting to be a national crisis.

'What did Owen think?' she asked innocently.

Owen had just enough sense to wriggle out of this one.

He had not given this the thought he should have done, he said, but, yes, there did seem to be some difficulties somewhere. There were always difficulties, for instance, with soldiers in barracks . . .

'Oh?' said Layla. 'What sort of difficulties?'

Owen refused to be trapped.

'Going back to the question of Marie,' he said.

Reluctantly, Layla abandoned this promising detour.

The nearest Marie had come to a boy friend was when, about a year ago, she had taken up with some students. It had all seemed to be going well, when the boy it seemed to be going particularly well with suddenly dropped out of the picture. Layla was not exactly sure why but thought he might have been warned off.

'By the Kewfiks?'

Layla thought so.

'I mean, they were big and he was small. They were rich and he was poor. I think if they had left it alone it would probably have petered out. But by making a fuss about it they gave it a new lease of life. They put up the backs of both of them. Marie and Ali, that was his name. Anyway, they chased him away and we didn't see anything of him for quite some time. But then the next thing we know, they were back together again. I think it was about that time that Marie took up music. Or maybe it was him, she took up him, and he played music, the *nay*, all the time . . . I don't know what she saw in him. There wasn't much conversation from him. Nor ideas for that matter, which she had been so interested in. I drifted away from her at that point. I mean, I like the *nay*, but a little of it goes a long way. She moved away from us generally. She said she had gone off men.'

A little later in the morning there was a tap on the door.

'Kewfik Effendi to see you,' said Nikos. 'He says it's urgent.'

'I thought he was in hospital?'

'No, it's the younger Kewfik. The nephew.'

'Show him in.'

Into the room came the old Harrowian.

'Owen, the most awful thing has come up!'

'Marie?'

'Yes. Absolutely awful!'

'Where did they find her?'

'What?'

'Where did they find the body? Presumably they found the body?'

'No, no, I don't think so.'

'What, then?' said Owen, puzzled.

'She hasn't a bean! Not a bean, old chap. It's all been spent. My uncle's financial wallah has been in to see me this morning. And, Owen, this is the most frightful thing: he is saying that I did it! Cleaned them out, that's what these financial wallahs are saying. Well, how was I to know? My father never told me! And now he's going absolutely mad! Blaming me, of all things!

"'Father, if it's anyone's fault, it's yours. I distinctly remember you telling me I could have what I wanted." "Help yourself, dear boy!" That's what he said. So I did. And now he's asking where it's all gone. That's hardly fair, is it? Anyway, those banking chaps ought to have told me. And they ought to have told him! Right at the start of all this. Then we'd have known where we stood. "I feel let down, Father, I really do!" That's what I told him.

'Here was I expecting a fortune, and making my dispositions accordingly, when it transpired that all the time there wasn't any money there! He ought to have been on top of this, he really ought. He waited until it had all gone and then he handed it over to me! "I'm sorry to say this, Father, but that's hardly honest of you!" That's what I told him, Owen. To his face.

'And do you know what he said? He practically accused me of having had my hand in the till! I may have occasionally helped myself to loose change, but that's all. And he never told me not to. And, anyway, it's ridiculous to say that I've cleaned them out! "There's plenty of money there." I distinctly remember him saying we were made for life. And another thing, what were those banker chaps doing? I thought they were supposed to be the experts. They ought to have kept an eye on it. I'll bet they're the ones who have been helping themselves at our expense! At my uncle's expense! At the expense of the whole family! "You ought to have stood

over them and made sure they were doing their job," I said. "Instead
you left it all for me to sort out. I call that very unhandsome."

'And what about this girl? This one who's got herself
kidnapped. "We can always fall back on her," he said. "We can
always marry her off to you." But what would be the point of
that, if she hasn't got any money? I asked the financial wallahs
about that this morning. "It's her money that you've spent," they
said. "No, no," I said, "her old man was always careful with
money. He put it aside for her and now, damn me, when we try
to put our hands on it, we find that it's not there!"

'And now they have the nerve to say that's because it's been
spent, and I am the one who has spent it! This is flagrant dishon-
esty! I shall take them through the courts. No, I won't! They're
as bad as the bankers. In fact, I'll bet they're in it with the
bankers: robbers, that's what they all are. And they're robbing
me! I know what it is. I'm not a fool, you know! They're setting
me up. They're shifting the blame on to me. They're all in it
together. My father has set me up, my uncle has set me up.
Everyone has set me up. I shall complain to the Khedive!

'I won't have it! I tell you, I won't have it! If there's a hole
in the money somewhere, then they just have to fill it. This is
not some little barber we're talking about, it's the Kewfiks!

'I tell you, we've got money. Loads of it. And if we don't
have the ready, we can call it in. And if we can't call it in, I
could always – well, yes, I could, at a pinch, I could marry that
girl, for instance. My father always said that she was our insur-
ance.

'Except she's been kidnapped! They've lost her, just as they
have the rest of our money. "It's the *caracol* for you, my man,"
I said. "You and all the rest of them. Prison is where you ought
to be, my man, and where you will be as soon as I can fix it!
No money? I'll bet there is money, tucked away somewhere.
Well, you just produce it!" They can't hide my money away, just
for their own selfish ends.

'Owen, can't you do something? Flog the money out of them
or something?'

Owen clucked his tongue sympathetically and said he was
sorry to hear about Ali Osman's troubles. But were they his

troubles? How much of the Kewfik finances had been put in his charge?

Ali Osman did not know.

'There will be a record, surely?'

Ali Osman didn't know about that. His father had told him that from now on the family money was his responsibility and that was it.

'I daresay my uncle will have got it straight,' he said hopefully, 'before passing responsibility to my father.'

'Perhaps,' said Owen.

'My uncle is the sort of man who would have lawyers. Dozens of them!'

'Of course, he may not have been able to see to that since having his stroke.'

'What would happen in that case?'

'I'm afraid you'll have to ask the lawyers.'

'But won't that take some time?'

'Yes.'

'So, what shall I do for ready?'

'There are people in the souk who would advance you money.'

'Tried them,' said Ali Osman. 'In fact, I've tried them a lot lately.'

'There will always be someone willing to make you an advance.'

Ali Osman, reflecting on his more recent experience, was not quite so sure.

'And then, of course,' said Owen, 'there's the question of the ransom.'

'Ransom?'

'For Marie Kewfik.'

'Well, we can hardly pay that now, can we?'

'Her mother has, I gather, been drumming up financial support.'

'Has she? Well, that's worth looking into. Do you think she might be willing to divert some?'

'I doubt it. She's had to scrape around as it is. What there is, is earmarked for the ransom. If it turns out you have to pay it.'

'You mean we may not have to pay it?'

'If we catch the kidnappers, and succeed in freeing Marie, then you won't need to pay a ransom. That is, of course, what we are trying to do. But, naturally there's always the chance that things could go wrong.'

'And then what?'

'Well, they might kill Marie.'

'Hmm,' said Ali Osman. 'That's a bit drastic.'

'Yes.'

Ali Osman considered. Then he brightened up.

'But if that happened, we would keep the money.'

'Your aunt would have the money. She may not give it to you.'

'But I'm the senior member of the family now. The family money is now my responsibility. Wouldn't I be the one who decides what happens to it?'

'I doubt it,' said Owen.

FIVE

At last what he had been waiting for arrived.

It came in the unlikely form of a junior official from one of the banks, complete with fez and a short cane, to demonstrate his superiority to ordinary folk.

It was a simple request for Mamur Zapt to call, accompanied if possible by Ali Osman Kewfik Effendi; and as soon as he learned that additional fact, Owen knew exactly what it was about.

The Gamaliya Quarter, which was where the most imposing offices of the city were located, was a great mixture. The houses were old and large, but most of them had been divided up and converted into offices. The remains of the old Mameluke houses were still apparent though, if you looked up. The upper storeys had huge oriel windows with lattices of rich and ancient meshrebiya from the old days through which the ladies of the harem had in the past been able to look down on the streets below without being observed. The streets had overhanging wooden porches. The woodwork, there since time immemorial, had warped into picturesque shapes and was so polished, not by hand but by sand, that it positively shone. The doors opened out onto the streets and through them you could glimpse fine panelling and marble floors. After the noise and bustle of the streets, the insides of the houses were dark and cool and calm. An Albanian in his national dress came forward and ushered them in.

The men there had probably never spoken to the Mamur Zapt but they knew at once who he was.

'Honoured, Mamur Zapt!'

'And on me, too, the honour!'

He was shown into a large inner room smelling curiously of sultanas, with carpets, not tapestry, on the walls and a sunken fountain bubbling at one end.

'You know Kewfik Effendi, I expect?' Owen asked.

'We do indeed. How is your uncle, Kewfik Effendi?'

'Not too well. But recovering.'

'We are glad to hear it. And your father?'

'Taking a breather on the coast.'

'It would be nice if we could all do that, but that is not yet for us, is it, Mamur Zapt?'

'Alas, not,' said Owen.

'And your – cousin, is it? The poor girl who has been kidnapped?'

'We hope she is still well,' said Owen.

'As do we, Mamur Zapt. As do we.'

'Worth a bit, still,' said Ali Osman. 'If she is still alive.'

'For your sake, as well as hers, we hope that is so.'

'It is, of course, on that business that we have come.'

'Of course. And if we could help you, we would. But I doubt if there is much that we can do.'

'You received a note from the kidnappers?'

'That is so, yes.'

'Why did it come to you?'

'They must have known that we were the Kewfiks' bankers.'

'How was the note presented?'

'At the door. The janitor took it in.'

'What was said?'

'I wasn't there. But enough for it to be taken at once to our president.'

'Money was demanded?'

'Yes. The bank refused. It said it would do nothing without authorisation. That is our standard procedure.'

'And their response?'

'Another message was sent, which said that it would be the worse for the girl if they did not get what they wanted.'

'And you said, that may be, but that without proper authorisation you would do nothing.'

There was a thin smile.

'The Mamur Zapt has met these situations before.'

'Indeed, he has. Did you arrange a subsequent meeting?'

'No, but we said one would be necessary.'

'You, too, have been in this situation before.'

'Alas, yes.'

'You are doing well. Keep playing them, but let us know.'

'There are dangers.'

'Yes. The principal one is that they might panic.'

'We will play them as long as we can. But the danger increases.'

'So negotiations cannot be prolonged too much. Nevertheless, prolonging is important. It gives us time.'

'We shall do our best.' The man paused. 'I have a daughter of my own,' he said.

'So have I. And that is why we cannot let it go on too long.'

The man inclined his head.

'It is good you have experience,' he said. 'When I did this before, I was young and inexperienced, as was everyone on our side, and so were they. The child died.'

'We will try to see that doesn't happen. Give the impression if you can that we are willing to meet their demands. It is just that we have to be sure of the details.'

The man nodded.

'We will do our best. We always do the best that we can for our customers.'

'Keep negotiating. Say that the father is in hospital and that the uncle is old. Say, perhaps, that it is necessary to go through the mother. Say that she loves her daughter and will agree but that it takes her time to understand. They will believe that, thinking that the nature of women.'

'They have not met my wife! But, yes, they probably will believe that.'

'Tell them we are doing all we can to hurry things up. Tell them they can be confident of success. But that if harm comes to the child, the family will spare no money in tracking them down.'

'It would be well to say that the Mamur Zapt cares particularly about this case and will spare nothing to ensure that, if anything goes wrong, they will certainly receive curious punishments. That, too, they will believe.'

'We understand each other, I think,' said Owen.

'We will do all we can. As I said, I have a daughter of my own.'

He hesitated.

'If we could whet the appetite a little, it could help.'

'Pay something in advance, you mean?'

'A little, yes. A very little, to show that we are serious. Not too much, however. Otherwise they will think we are easy.'

'Can that be arranged?'

'Yes. Perhaps, though we had better make it a specific sum. The amount, we leave to you.'

'Could we agree on who is handling it on your side? Yourself, preferably. The fewer people in on this the better.'

'I will handle it personally.'

'Thank you.'

'And on your side?'

'Not me personally. Do it through my man, Nikos. Do you know him? Nikos the Copt.'

'We know him. A good man of business!'

'That is why it will be done through him. Not everyone, I will let you in on a secret, at the Bab-el-Khalk, is good with money, and I say that with confidence, for I myself am not good with money – or so our Accounts department tell me.'

The men from the bank laughed.

'In return, I will tell you a secret, Captain Owen. My boss doesn't understand a thing about money. But what he does understand is the politics of money. And I think you are like that. For the people at the top may not know much about the details but what they understand only too well is that all in the end, all finance, is a matter of politics, and all politics is in the end a matter of finance.'

As they were going away, Ali Osman said: 'Is that true, do you think? That in the end all politics is a matter of finance; and all finance is a matter of politics?'

'More or less, yes.'

They walked on in silence for a little while. Then Ali Osman said: 'You know, Owen, I'm not sure I want to be in charge of the family finances, or of the family either!'

Owen clasped him round the shoulders.

'Why Ali Osman, I think we'll make you fit to run the Kewfik estate yet.'

Owen had invited Layla to come and see him. Layla responded with alacrity; not just because she sensed it was to do with Marie, but also because she quite liked the idea of being, as she supposed, at the centre of things. In fact, when she arrived he had just been phoned by the Consul-General and was tied up in a conversation with him.

'Sorry,' he said to Layla. 'Would you mind waiting, just for a minute? It's important or I wouldn't bother.'

Layla sat quietly for a while but then began to move around straightening things and looking at others, especially the books. Mostly they were government reports, bound in the usual grey government paper. Layla picked out one and began to read. It was the Annual Report of the Sanitation Department, which was important in a place like Cairo, and Owen had been meaning to get around to reading it for quite some time. Layla was curious about the way government worked and soon became absorbed.

Nikos came in and stood looking at her, irritated by her presence.

He returned some of the things she had touched to their original places. Layla barely looked up from the report. A moment later, without registering her actions, she picked up some of the papers Nikos had moved and put them back where she had placed them.

Nikos looked at her in fury.

'There are principles, you know! If you move things, I shan't be able to tell him where to find them.'

'Pardon?' said Layla, noting his disapproval.

'There is a system!' said Nikos.

'Oh, sorry! It just looked a bit of a mess, that was all.'

'A woman cannot be expected to understand these things,' said Nikos loftily.

'Understand what?' said Layla, closing her book.

'This is not women's work. It is men's work.'

Which, in Egypt, it was.

'If I was doing it,' said Layla thoughtfully, 'I'd put the most recent reports over here. Then you'd be able to put his hands on them straightaway.'

'Well, you're not doing it,' said Nikos. 'I am!'

'But if I were—' said Layla.

'What's all this?' asked Owen, coming in.

'She's telling me how to do my job!' said Nikos.

'No, I'm not,' said Layla, 'I'm just making a few suggestions for improvements.'

Nikos stalked out.

'I've hurt his feelings,' said Layla contritely.

'They get hurt regularly. He'll survive.'

'Do you think being a secretary is a man's work?' asked Layla. 'I'm in two minds. In some ways I think it's a man's work. It always has been a man's job, at least in the Ottoman Empire. But should it be? It's a job women could do just as well, if not better. But then, if men didn't do jobs like this, what jobs would they do? They can't all be bricklayers.'

'I ask myself what job I would do,' said Owen. 'I wouldn't be much good as a bricklayer, but then, I don't think I would be much good as a secretary, either.'

'All you can be is a boss,' said Layla. 'Oh, you poor thing!'

Owen laughed.

'Now,' he said, 'there is something I want to ask you.'

'Ask away.'

'You said Marie's boy friend had come back to Cairo?'

'Yes.'

'Where will I find him?'

'I can't tell you that,' protested Layla indignantly. 'It wouldn't be right.'

'It might help find Marie.'

'I don't think he knows.'

'All the same. I'd like to talk to him.'

'Well, I don't think I can help you.'

'Why not?'

Layla considered.

'It'd be a bit like betrayal,' she said.

'It might help us to find Marie.'

'Well . . .'

'Are you more of a friend of his than you are Marie's?'

'Of course not!'

'Then why won't you tell me where he is? I'm not going to hurt him. All I want to do is talk to him.'

'We know that kind of talk!'

'I'm not going to knock him about, if that's what you are thinking.'

'Well, no. I don't suppose you are. But he might say something and you might pass it on, and then there might be someone who would knock him about.'

'It happens more rarely than you might think.'

'It happens more commonly than you, away in your office, might suppose.'

'All I want to do is talk to him. And because what he has to say might affect our chance of finding Marie, I shall be very careful about how I use the information. And if I tell anyone else about what he has said, which I may not do, they'll know it's on a confidential basis and that I will hold them to account if any word gets out. The whole point of any inquiry of this sort is that it has to be done very quietly. Otherwise there may be repercussions to Marie.'

'I don't like it being secret. It worries me.'

'It worries me, too, and I don't like having to work like that. But in a thing like kidnapping you have to. The biggest risk is that word gets out, of where you are and what you are going for. Because then they might panic and kill the person you're trying to save.'

'Why don't you just offer them money?'

'We are offering them money.'

'Offer them more!'

'We will.'

'They'll take it, won't they?'

'They'll ask for more.'

'Give them more.'

'We will. But one day there'll come a point when we can't or when it doesn't work. They'll get frightened and then run away. First dumping the evidence. Look, I don't believe Marie's friend is necessarily involved. But I do think it's more than likely that he's got some idea of the people who are. We want to know, and we need to know quickly, so I need to know what he knows.'

She was silent. Then she said, 'I hate this.'

'So do I, but sometimes it's necessary.'

'I used to think I wouldn't mind being Mamur Zapt. Now I don't want to.'

'I can understand that.'

'I used to blame the British for doing things like this. But it would happen if the British were no longer here, wouldn't it?'

'Yes, it would. The only difference would be that it would be an Egyptian doing what I'm doing.'

'That would be better.'

'It wouldn't be any easier, though. I have a friend who is in the Parquet. Sometimes he has to do things like this and he doesn't like it either. He agrees with you, but he also agrees with me. He hates this kind of work.'

'Why does he do it then? Why do you do it?'

Owen shrugged.

'Because someone has to do it, I suppose you'll say. Whether they're Egyptian or whether they're English. You should meet my friend.'

'I would like to.'

'Perhaps I'll introduce you. Yes, that's a good idea. I'll introduce you myself.'

Layla sat thinking. Then she said: 'There is a club they used to go to, it is called Serpent of the Nile. They used to go there because it played their kind of music. You know, traditional, folk music, that sort of thing. It's not the usual kind of club. It's not a student club but a more grown-up sort of club. That's why Marie and Ali liked it. They weren't interested in the usual student music. This music was special.'

Owen knew, or thought he knew, every club in Cairo. They were important to the life of the city. Restaurants often doubled up as clubs, and regulars, nearly always men, congregated there every evening to smoke (usually bubble pipes) and play dominoes. There was no drinking of course, Egypt being a Muslim country. There were less salubrious places, mostly frequented by the poorer kind of tourist (the richer kind went to the hotels where sometimes they could sit outside on a verandah and drink cocktails) and by British soldiers. These were policed by military policemen, who ejected trouble-makers, at least they did after three in the morning. Juke boxes were creeping in and sometimes music was provided by a singer, usually a black Nubian lady or a transsexual Levantine, but there weren't many bands. The great thing to be said for the men's clubs was that they were usually half underground and therefore dark and cool.

There were also very, very many student clubs, which were of quite a different sort, serving only fruit juice or tea. Popular drinks brands were only just creeping in and what was mainly drunk was a sickly lemonade. The tables were long and low and served mainly as gathering points for conversations.

The main business of the student clubs was talk: usually political, often radical and sometimes revolutionary. The police kept an eye on them, not because the behaviour was disorderly but because the talk was. Among the British civil servants there were two opinions about them: one was that they fomented trouble and should be put down; the other that they siphoned off trouble and diverted it into colourful but harmless outlets. Owen inclined to the latter view.

Nikos kept a list of the most insurrectionary ones, but it was always having to be updated as student organisations came and went with astonishing speed.

The Serpent of the Nile was a new one on Owen. It was small and tucked away up a side street and to get to it you went down a flight of steps. Since it was a student club, Owen had taken the precaution of going with the son of an Egyptian colleague, which had the additional advantage that he knew Shawquat and would be able to identify him. Shawquat was not actually there when Owen arrived but his companion said that he might come later: 'when things hotted up'. The place was already crowded. The son said that it was because there would be a good singer tonight. He added that they were in luck because it was a singer whom the young Shawquat especially favoured. He went to most of her performances. She was, said his companion, not the tummy-wriggling popular performer of the lower clubs but a proper alimeh or awalim, or 'learned female'. Owen was pleased because you didn't often get the chance to hear a true awalim. This was music for the connoisseur.

She was tall and thin and dressed in the traditional black, although without a veil. From all around the room when she came in there were appreciative cries. She acknowledged them modestly. No showwoman she.

There was a small dais at one end of the room, on to which she climbed. A troupe of musicians followed her in and sat at the back. There was an 'ood, a kind of lute, played with a plectrum (made from a vulture's feather), and a nay, which required considerable skill in the playing, and also a rikk, a small tambourine.

She looked around the room imperiously and then began to

sing, in the quavering voice, and with the distinct enunciation, of the true Arabic singer, precise and not overdone. What she was singing, Owen realised after a moment, were traditional Arab folksongs.

Oh, you beauties of Alexandria!
Your walk over the furniture is alluring.
You wear the Kashmir shawl,
And your lips are sweet as sugar.

Owen always liked the walk-over-the furniture bit, which was a product of the usual Lane translation, and which he took to be referring to the carpets being on the floor and not, as they usually were, on the wall.

She had just started her second song when Owen's companion gave him a nudge. A young man had just come in and pushed himself through to the front row of the audience. He was sitting right beside the tambourine player, whom he seemed to know. They exchanged glances and then, for a moment, the incomer was allowed a pat on the tambourine.

The awalim sang several songs, each rapturously received, and then stepped down off the dais and went out. As she passed Shawquat she touched him lightly on the head.

She came back later and sang some more songs, each one traditional and beautifully sung. The audience was in raptures and even Owen found himself drawn in. This time, as she left, she touched the young Shawquat on the shoulder. It was an affectionate rather than an inviting smile.

And then, as she walked out of the room she turned, crossed the room to where Owen was sitting and unmistakably beckoned him. This surprised those sitting around Owen and there was a little stir. The awalim ignored it, however, and went out. As she went, she glanced back, and Owen knew he was meant to follow.

The room was tiny and already occupied. As they entered, a woman stood up and threw a shawl around the awalim's shoulders. From somewhere she produced a glass of water and then stood behind the awalim gently massaging her temples and throat.

The awalim looked up at Owen.

'The Kewfik girl,' she said, 'she is alive and well. The old women of the souk send this message.'

'Tell them I am grateful,' said Owen. 'I am grateful to them, and to you for bearing the message, and also to Allah, if the message be true.'

'Are you?' said the awalim.

'Am I . . .?' said Owen, slightly taken aback, it was as if she was challenging him.

'To Allah?'

'To a general Allah,' said Owen.

The awalim smiled.

'That, I think, is different. I, too, bless a general Allah,' said the awalim.

'Don't we all, when it comes down to it?'

'Very probably. Nevertheless, I am grateful to whichever of the Allahs it is from whom the message comes. Truly grateful, for I feared for the Kewfik girl.'

'Why?'

'Does one have to explain why one fears for a child?'

'To me, you do. I have no child.'

'Will it offend you, if I say that I am sorry?'

The awalim smiled and took another sip of water.

Then she said: 'The girl is not here.'

'But the Shawquat boy is.'

'He is always here.'

'Why?'

'He likes the old music. He would like to sing it. He has a good ear but his voice is not good enough.'

'He would like to learn it?'

She made a gesture of dismissal.

'It is out of the question.'

'And the girl: would she like to learn it also?'

'I think she is more interested in the boy than in the music.'

'Where he goes, she goes?'

The awalim nodded.

'In fact, she has a nice voice, but she does not wish to use it. It does not matter. Only some can be singers, but all can listen.'

'Apart from this boy, she came here to listen?'

'To learn to listen. It is not something you do casually. My friend in the souk wants her to learn the music properly. The old music. Unless new people learn, young people, the knowledge will fade away. When I go, who will sing after me? The young

Shawquat, for example. But his mind is so full of other things as well that he gets confused and will lose his way. This is true of the young in general. They are confused and so the country loses its way.'

She stood up, and her attendant removed the shawl from around her shoulder.

'It is good to talk to you,' she said. 'I do not often have the chance to talk much about such things. I talk, of course, with my friend, and with other awalim but they talk in the same old way. This is why my friend likes to talk to the young. Fresh young minds see things freshly. She says that is what will change Egypt.'

Owen stood outside the club waiting for Ali Shawquat to come out. He was thinking, first about the music, the awalim's singing. It stayed with him; he began to realise how unusual and beautiful it was. He had never heard singing like it before. Mahmoud had sometimes spoken about it – he and Aisha were lovers of the old, traditional folk music, and before their children came on the scene they used to go regularly to hear it – but Owen had never quite taken it in. Somehow, he had gone through Egypt deaf. Of course, he had heard music going on in the background, over the radio, in the clubs, among men working in the fields or on the dahabeeahs sailing on the river, but in the background and he had never paid much attention. But the music he had heard tonight deserved attention. And not just for its qualities as music but for what it was saying. It was talking about the country Egypt had been but also about the country it could become. This was political stuff. How could he, who lived for Egypt's political stuff, have missed it? It had been there, deep down, all the time and he had not been listening. It was a great, buried Egypt beginning to stir.

The other thing he noticed as he stood there waiting for Ali Shawquat to emerge was how much it had to do with women. It was there in what the awalim sang. But it was also there in other things, in the many things that women did that sustained the life of the community. You never saw them behind their burkas but they were an invisible army working away all the time. You saw them going about their business, hidden behind their long veils, carrying their baskets of vegetables, often on their head, their sticks and circles of bread, their children on one hip, a great pot of water on the other. An unknown multitude behind their burkas and it was they who carried life on.

And they were beginning to stir. They were beginning to come out from behind their veils and say something. That was what the awalim's singing was all about. It was there in the voices of the young. The girls of the Khedivial, for example. Bright, lively and questioning. If revolution came to Egypt it would come from them. The Laylas and Maries, yes, and in the future, perhaps, the Minyas.

It was a thought that had not really struck home before. Men didn't see women in Egypt. They shrank into the background. Men took them for granted. But would they be able to do so when girls like Layla grew up?

There was movement at the back door of the club and several people came out. Among them was the Shawquat boy. Owen went across to him and put his arm loosely around his shoulders in the intimate Arab way. In the darkness Ali took it for the action of a friend and went with it as Owen pulled him away from the group.

'Greetings, Ali Shawquat.'

'And to your greetings,' the Egyptian replied automatically, and then looked at Owen and pulled away.

Owen tightened his clasp.

'Who are you?'

'A friend.'

'I don't think I know you,' said the Egyptian suspiciously.

'I am a friend of Marie Kewfik.'

'Marie!' said the boy, and then, unexpectedly burst into tears.

'How is Marie?'

'I – I don't know.'

'How is that? She was with you.'

'She was with me but – they took her away!'

'So where is she now?'

'I – I don't know.'

'Is she all right?'

'Yes, yes!'

'Where is she?'

'She is with . . . friends.'

'No, she is not. She is with enemies. Tell me.'

'She is with enemies, yes. But – but they won't hurt her!'

'How do you know that?'

'They – they want money.'

'From the Kewfiks?'

'Yes.'

'And they will hold her until they get the money?'

'Yes.'

'How do you know that?'

'That is what they said.'

'They said, when?'

'When they took her.'

'You were with her when they took her?'

'Yes. I – I tried to stop them but there were too many for me. They knocked me to the ground and stood over me. And when I looked up, Marie was gone and I shouted and cried out to them. But they bade me be silent or harm would befall me and her.'

'They took her when she was walking with you: how was that?'

'I couldn't stop them! They were many and I was but one.'

'But they knew you would be walking together?'

'Yes, we always walked home together. After music.'

'Music?'

'Yes. I used to play after school. In the playground. People wanted me to play, so I did, every day. And Marie came and listened to me. And then, at the end, when I had finished playing, we went home together.'

'So they knew you would be walking home together at this time?'

'Yes.'

'You did it regularly?'

'Yes, I used to walk her home to her house, but not go in. The Kewfiks have a big house on the edge of the Geziret but I would not go in. They were too great for me.'

'But they knew that you walked home together?'

'They had watched me.'

'Having seen that was what you did regularly.'

'Yes.'

He nodded and looked down at the ground.

'And perhaps I had boasted.'

'Boasted?'

'About Marie. She was great and I was little and I was proud. Proud that she would have to do with one such as me. And I boasted about it. I am ashamed now. Very ashamed. I am evil!'

'Did you do bad things with her?'

'No! Never! I've asked but she won't let me. She said: "When you are famous then it can happen but not until then." I would have kissed her but she pushed me away. But I did not mind that. I do not wish to treat her lightly. For me she is – a superior being, superior in all respects. Beautiful, and kind, and good. I want to be with her for ever. And I thought I could make it so with my *nay*. I am a good player, I know I am a good player. And she believes in me! I know, with her beside me, I can be a success. We speak of it often, of when we could be together. With her beside me, I – I will work harder. I can feel myself becoming better. As a musician you know these things, and I know I can do it. I can become worthy of her, and worthy of the music that speaks through me. Not all the time, only sometimes. But sometimes there is a flash and I can feel it inside me. And when it comes out I say: "Only you could do this!" and I think: when I am famous they will let me marry her! And so we dream together!'

'How came it about that you fell in with evil men?'

'They heard me playing. I used to play at school. At lunchtime or after school, when we had finished for the day. Of course, I wasn't playing what I play now. Then, I used to play, well, what children like. Now I play the old songs. The awalim teaches me. She sings and I play. The songs are not written down, you have to learn them by ear. And then, of course, you have to shift them to make them suitable for the *nay*. Well, I can do that, not everybody can. But I can do it well. Sometimes I gather with other musicians and we listen to a song and then we play it among ourselves and come to remember it. Only we don't all remember it in the same way. An *'ood* player remembers it differently from a *nay* player. And then we all come together and there is a singer as well, and it is beautiful. Perhaps someday I will play some of them to you—'

'I would like that,' said Owen.

'Marie likes that too. We go together to places like the Serpent and I would listen to the *nay* player and learn the songs. And then go through them with Marie.'

'You would do this together?'

'We did, yes, and it was wonderful!'

'Why, then did you betray her?'

'Betray her?'

'You boasted of her. And drew the attention of those bad men to her.'

The boy didn't say anything for a while. Then he said: 'It is true. I shamed her and shamed myself and in doing so, God forgive me, brought about her kidnapping.'

'Why did you do this?'

'I lost touch with myself. My true self. My true self loves Marie and plays music. But at the time there were so many other things going on about me. It seemed that the whole world was waking. A new Egypt was coming into being and we all wanted to be part of it. So we threw stones. It was childish, I know, but we wanted to do something to show that we were part of this awakening. Now, the men egged us on. And then, when we wanted to stop, when we did stop, they sneered at us. "Is that all you can do?" they said.

'And then they turned to me. "You go with that Kewfik girl," they said. "What do you do with her? Do you do with her what a man does?" and I, God forgive me, said, "Yes." But it wasn't true. She's never let me, and I – well, for me she is holy. I would never wrong her. Never!'

He began to cry.

'And yet you let them take her.'

'What could I do? They were many and I was but one. But, yes, I should have done something. I could have done something. But I was frightened, and it all happened so quickly, and when it came to it I did nothing, God forgive me! I did not even speak of it. I could have spoken of it to you, couldn't I? But, to my shame I did not. Afterwards I wanted to kill myself. I still want to kill myself. If anything happens to her, I *shall* kill myself!'

He buried his face in his hands and tears were running down his face. 'Let me die!' he said. 'Please let me die!'

SIX

Minya came skipping through the school gates, singing. She came to the main road, stopped, and looked both ways, as Marie had instructed her to. Far away in the distance there was an arabeah coming towards her but it was still too far away to be a danger. She continued skipping and singing, across the road, and there, on the far side, was the nice policeman.

'Why, it's my little pigeon!' said Selim, affecting surprise.

Then he scooped her up and carried her a little way, through the next crossroads before setting her down. Walking Minya home was no longer officially part of Selim's duties but he saw it as a legitimate extension of them. Besides, only that morning he had seen a badmash lurking about near the school gates and decided to keep his eye on him.

Minya continued carolling.

'What is that you are singing?' asked Selim.

Minya continued.

'The perfection of your eyes has quite overthrown me!'

Selim joined in.

'. . . *and the music has increased my madness, I am left bereft and weeping!'*

'Why is he weeping?' asked Minya.

'Because it is all so beautiful,' said Selim. 'His heart overflows.'

'Does your heart overflow?' asked Minya.

'Sometimes,' said Selim. 'When it is nice music. Although not as often as it used to.'

'It's not my heart,' said Minya. 'It's my feet. When I hear lovely music I want to skip.'

'I might,' said Selim. 'But it's one thing you skipping and it's another thing me skipping!'

'Perhaps you could dance,' suggested Minya. 'Men do that sometimes.'

'I can still jump in the air,' said Selim.

'I'll bet you can jump really high!'

'Pretty high,' said Selim modestly.

'Go on. Show me!'

Selim gave a mighty bound.

Minya clapped her hands.

Selim was about to repeat his bound when he realised that the arabeah had caught up with them and the arabeah driver was watching with interest.

Selim converted the bound into a shuffle and then into a nonchalant walk.

'Got children of my own!' said the arabeah driver sympathetically.

Selim dropped Minya off at what had become a familiar point near her house and went on his way. Then, ahead of him, he saw a little group of people standing around a recumbent form lying in the road.

One of the figures turned to him.

'You'd better get the Parquet,' he said.

Selim looked at the motionless figure.

Yes, it was definitely a matter for the Parquet, and not for the hospital. He thought he'd better stay by the figure, and sent one of the bystanders to report the matter at the offices.

Then he turned his attention back to the prone figure. The man was an ordinary working man, dressed in galabiya. There was a big patch of blood on his back. Neither the prone figure nor the patch of blood were uncommon things in this part of Cairo.

'Any idea who he is?' he asked the people standing around.

'He works at the Kewfiks.'

Kewfik? It wasn't just that the name rang a bell it would anywhere in Cairo, but it rang a particular bell with Selim just at the moment. He didn't know much about Marie's kidnapping but he knew that his little pigeon was something to do with it, and that was enough.

'At the Kewfiks?' he said.

'Yes. In the stables.'

And now that it had been mentioned, there was a definite whiff of the stables in the air. Selim looked at the man's hands and that confirmed it.

He sent another man to the Bab-el-Khalk.

*   *   *

Owen was talking to Georgiades when the messenger arrived. They both, of course, knew Selim, and while they had great respect for his physical strength and ability, this did not extend to mental gymnastics. Nevertheless, on a thing like this they respected his judgement.

'Want me to go?' asked Georgiades.

Owen nodded; and went with him.

The small knot of figures was still standing there when they arrived.

Georgiades bent over him.

'It's as it looks,' he said to Owen. 'A stab wound in the back, by an expert, I would say.'

But then most of the wounds in this part of Cairo were. Nor were such incidents uncommon. In fact, there was nothing to detain their attention. Except for the name.

'Kewfik,' he said.

'Worked in the stables,' someone offered.

'I'll go along,' said Georgiades.

Owen nodded.

He stood there for a moment looking around him.

'Anyone see it happen?' he asked.

No one had, but then in this part of Cairo that, too, was not unusual.

'Who found him?'

Two of the bystanders put their hands up.

'Both of you? Together?'

It was always as well, in these streets, and with these witnesses, to have some corroboration.

They had they said, just been to the souk, independently, and been walking along the Sharia Hara en Nabawiyeh – yes, to the Tribunal Indigence et Prisons, and what was wrong with that? – when they had seen this man lying in the road. At first they had assumed that he had been knocked over by an arabeah, these arabeah drivers drove like lunatics, and had gone over to help (and search through his pockets) when they saw the wound on his back and decided to get out of it quickly. But other men had come by this time and it was too late to get out of it unwitnessed, and, besides, there was much to talk about. And then this policeman had come along and started asking questions and they had given their names and now it was much too late, and, besides, it was obviously the hand of God and there was not much that anyone could do.

Who was it that recognised that the man had worked for the Kewfiks?

It was Alou, and Alou was produced, and, though overcome by the fame suddenly thrust upon him, confirmed that he had recognised the man. He worked in the Kewfik stables. Alou's sister's friend's cousin worked there too and they knew each other. Not well, he added hastily, just a passing acquaintance, and now passing on the other side of the street.

By now, probably thanks to Georgiades, the Kewfik house had been informed, and a woman came flying up the street towards them and threw herself upon the body. She, it turned out, was the dead man's wife, or would have been his wife if they had got round to it. Certainly there were children, lots, the number growing all the time, and could the Effendi—

No, the Effendi, although boundlessly sympathetic, could not. Anyway, the body had to be certified first, and that was a job for the Parquet.

Who was this, then? The Mamur Zapt. Well, now, that was different. Half the bystanders hurriedly went away, and the other half crowded round the dead man's wife, who, of course, had been standing there for some time.

It was, that is, what happened every day in Cairo streets: a body, a crowd within seconds, much excitement, a million words and not a hard fact among them.

Owen moved away. Out of the corner of his eye he saw a man in a smart suit and a natty red fez coming along the street towards them and knew it was the Parquet and that investigation should be handed over to them. The Mamur Zapt was not concerned with everyday crime in the streets, but only with political crime. And the only indication that this was a political crime at all was the name Kewfik; and that might just be an accident.

However, he didn't think it was.

Georgiades was in the stables. As befitted such a great family, they were large. The Kewfiks ran to several carriages. At the moment hardly any were in use. The man of the house was in hospital. The wives were all tucked away in interior rooms, no doubt talking about the murdered stablehand. The servants were standing around outside where it was cooler. Two of the men, however, unliveried and with shovels in their hands, were talking. Not very animatedly, since this was just a minor stablehand and of no importance. Georgiades went up to them.

'Just seen one of your chaps,' he said.

'Oh, yes?'

'He was dead.'

'That would be Ishaq.'

'I was coming along to tell you, but you've heard already then?'

'Man came ten minutes ago.'

'Knifed.'

'Another one. We've told Abdullah.'

'Abdullah is your boss, is he?'

'Yes, and he'll be hopping mad. Another one! That's two in the last week! He'll be looking around for men if it goes on like this! And there was one last week, and another one the week before. It's a good job the carriages are not much in use just now.'

'The horses are still shitting, though.'

'That's true.'

'And we're still shovelling.'

'And that's true, too.'

'Did I hear right?' said Georgiades. 'Four men in the last three weeks. That's a lot!'

'Four, yes, that's right. Or wasn't there another one?'

'Are you counting Ali?'

'Yes.'

'Why so many?' asked Georgiades. 'Is there a war on?'

'Sort of. It's us against the Kauri boys.'

'Well, it doesn't look as if you're doing too well.'

'You should see them!'

'I haven't heard anything about this.'

'Well, you wouldn't. There was trouble in the souk last week and one or two people got hurt. It was us against the Kauri boys. And then the police stopped us and sorted them both out. And now it's gone quiet because Abdullah says that with the Pasha in hospital, his wife, the senior wife, that is, doesn't like trouble. So we're holding our horses, so to speak, so I suppose the Kauri lads are doing the same. The bimbashi has been after them.'

'About time too! They cause all the trouble.'

'Ah, but do they?' said Georgiades. 'Some people were saying that it was your lot that had started it.'

'Oh, no, come on—'

'That's what they said.'

'It's a pack of lies. He came to pieces in my hands!' said one man, laughing.

'Abdullah says, don't let it happen again. Not for the next week or two, anyway.'

The stables of the big Pashas were always at loggerheads, Georgiades knew that. But what had led to this latest outbreak?

Owen had let Ali Shawquat go. The musician seemed harmless enough, but Owen had warned him to stay in the area, near or in the family house. Their chances of making contact with Marie's kidnappers, and Marie herself might depend on this. The broken *nay* player had assured him that he would. He had failed Marie when the kidnappers had surrounded them and taken Marie away but he would not, he swore, fail her again.

'Be it so!' said Owen sternly, and he thought that the boy meant it. If he was contacted by anyone about the kidnapping, he was to inform Owen immediately. He thought it unlikely that the kidnappers would, but in his experience, having found a weak spot, criminals would often come back to it. He didn't see why they should in this case but was anxious to guard against the possibility, and to exploit it if it should occur.

He checked up and found that the boy had indeed returned home. The activity brought back into his mind Ali Shawquat's father, who, he remembered now, worked at the Kewfik stables. He sent a message to Georgiades to look out for him. The message came back that the elder Shawquat had not been seen at the stables for several days now.

Owen decided to call on the family himself. The boy was there but not the father, nor was the mother. She was at the well drawing water. Owen intercepted her and asked her where her husband was. The woman was obviously shaken by this inquiry but replied that she did not know. He was out of town, visiting relatives. When asked about the address of this relative, she became confused.

Owen sat down on the parapet of the well, to make clear that this might turn out to be no short-term inquiry and that therefore she would do better to speak up at once. After some hesitation she said that he was not with a relative after all but at a meeting.

Could she give the place of this meeting? Eventually, she could – it was at a house in another part of Cairo, the district headquarters of a union that he belonged to.

Owen warned her to speak the truth, for he would check. 'Go on and check then!' she said, and he was reminded that she had struck him, when they had met previously, as a strong woman. He thought he would try to soften her, so reminded her that he was seeking help in finding Marie Kewfik. She knew about Marie's relationship with her son, the music player, had, indeed, spoken with him and found him helpful. So why should not she be?

'The Kewfiks have never done anything for us,' said the woman.

'They have given your man a job,' said Owen, 'isn't that something?'

'And they'd take it away at once if it suited them!'

He tried another approach.

'Your son, I think, loves her. That at any rate is what he says.' She bit her lip.

'It would be better if he had never set eyes on her!'

'It is too late now,' said Owen.

'No,' she said, 'it is not too late. It will not come to anything.'

'Not if she is in bad men's hands.'

'The Kewfiks are not for us,' she said adamantly.

'Probably not. But your families have touched and that cannot be undone now. Besides, a daughter is a daughter. Who would want her harmed?'

'Who would wish her good? No one around here.'

'Come,' said Owen. 'She is but a child. Your son is still but a child. Why should you and I wish harm on children?'

'It is nothing to do with us,' said the woman. 'It is nothing to do with you, either. This is not your country.'

'No,' said Owen. 'But while we are here, it is. And, while we are here, I wish harm neither on your son nor on the Kewfiks.'

'They wish harm on us.'

'Does the girl wish harm? Does your son wish harm?'

'The boy is a milksop. He lives in a dream. He throws stones with the others but that is all.'

She looked up.

'My man comes,' she said.

A short, grey-haired man in a beaded skullcap had come into the square. He saw them and came across to them.

'This man wishes to speak to you,' said his wife.

'Speak on, then. Is it about the boy?'

'I have spoken to the boy. There seems no reason to speak to him more.'

'Oh! Good, then.'

'It is you I wish to speak to. You have been away from the stables today, so perhaps you have not heard. A man from the stables has been killed.'

Shawquat shrugged.

'Another one,' he said.

'Yes. Another one. There have been too many.'

'Speak to the Kauris, then.'

'That is what I am going to do. But I thought I would speak to you first.'

'Perhaps this is wise. For then you will hear the truth.'

'The truth has many sides and I wish to hear all.'

'There is always trouble between the Kauris and the Kewfiks. Sometimes it flares up and sometimes it doesn't. But it is always there.'

'Why?'

The man shrugged again.

'It always has been there,' he said, as if no further explanation was needed.

'Why has it flared up again now?'

Shawquat shrugged.

'A word, perhaps? A jest? Or a blow.'

'Do words or jests lead to killings?'

'Sometimes they do.'

'But usually they don't. Why should they do so now?'

'Ask the Kauris.'

'I will. But now I am asking you. I ask man to man. Reply man to man.'

'It is not man to man if the English are one side of the conversation.'

'It will be you who stops it from being man to man.'

'Oh, yes?' said Shawquat, with an approach to a sneer.

Owen saw that resistance was setting in. He shifted tack.

'I have heard that it began with the stone throwing in the souk. Your son was part of the stone throwing. Why was that?'

'Someone put him up to it.'

'They say he is not one to throw stones lightly.'

'He is not,' agreed Shawquat.

'He makes music.'

'To my shame,' said Shawquat.

'Music making is shameful now, is it?'

'He should be studying, for a start. I have to find money for him to live while he studies. I do not find money for him to play the *nay*.'

'Nor to take the Kewfiks' girl to hear him play?'

'Nor that. Above all, not that!'

'Why not?'

'They are our enemies. The rich. When I heard that he had been throwing stones in the souk, my heart lifted. At last! I said. At last he is doing something worthy.'

'Worthy?'

'Of a man.'

'Do you throw stones?'

'I have done. Now I throw stones in other ways. Would to God he would do that! But he just plays his *nay*. It is not what a man should do. What would his grandfather say? He would feel ashamed. And I feel ashamed. He shames the whole family!'

'Do the men at the stables speak of him?'

He started.

'Do they?' he said.

Owen said nothing.

'If they do,' said Shawquat, 'I will kill them.'

'I have not heard them speak of him.'

'But they might! They might!'

'Calm yourself. I speak only of possibilities. And what I am trying to do is see how the girl might fit with this. Do the men at the stables speak of her?'

'There is always talk.'

'And is the talk fanned by what is happening between the two of them? The rich girl and the stable boy?'

'There is talk. How could there not be? I have spoken to him. I said: "This will not do! This will lead to trouble!"'

'Was not your son sent away? Because of this?'

Shawquat did not reply at once. Then he said, 'Yes.'

'Was that your doing? Or the Kewfik family's?'

He did not reply at once, and so Owen repeated the question.

'Theirs,' whispered Shawquat after a moment.

Then he burst out: 'They sent a man to me. And he said: "This will end in trouble. For you and your son. Let us ward it off. We will help you . . ." I spoke to Ali. And they spoke to a college far off. Ali moved. The Kewfiks have power. They can bring about these things. Ali went away. It was better like that. There would have been trouble. A family like mine cannot afford to meddle with the rich. It was better that way.'

'But then he came back?'

'It was her doing, not his.'

'He came back; and the talk began again?'

When he got back to his office, he found that the Khedivial girls were taking action.

'We cannot leave it to anyone else,' said Layla. 'It is wrong not to be doing anything. And that means us! I am sure you are doing your best, but it is all so slow!'

'So what do you propose to do?'

What they proposed to do soon became apparent, as the wide Midan in front of the Bab-el-Khalk began to fill up with school-girls. Nikos was in a state of shock. He retired to his office and locked the door.

'We won't be here long,' apologised Layla. 'This is just an assembly point.'

'And afterwards?'

'We move to the Midan Abdin.'

The Palace Square.

'It is bigger than the Bab-el-Khalk,' said Layla. 'We had thought of assembling there in the first place. But we thought that if we assemble in small groups they would find it easy to disperse us. If we have already got together in a mass they will it find it harder to do anything about us. And, besides, we'll be more conspicuous in front of the Palace. We spoke to Bimbashi McPhee, who is an old sweetie, but he wasn't happy about us being right in front of the Palace. He said, "What would the Khedive think?" We said that was just the point. We wanted to get the Khedive thinking, and everyone else, about Marie. It is disgraceful that in a civilized country like Egypt people can get away with kidnapping a schoolgirl and nobody's doing anything about it! Oh, I know you are, behind the scenes. But you don't seem to be getting anywhere. And it is important that people *see* things are happening, that we are not going to allow kidnappers to get away with doing whatever they like.'

'I take your point. What worries me though is that the kidnappers may become as frightened of you as I am and that there could be consequences for Marie.'

'You'll be working behind the scenes, remember? And we'll be working in front of them. We'll both be working together. That will take some of the heat out of the situation.'

'I suppose I couldn't just forbid you to go ahead with demonstrating?'

'No, you can't,' said Layla.

Owen wondered if he could persuade them to move the demonstration to the other side of the Nile, or, preferably, into the Nile.

Meanwhile, the numbers in the Bab-el-Khalk were swelling. They filed into the Midan with enviable discipline and stood in their ranks quietly. It was uncanny. He was sure he couldn't do as well. Here they were, all in neat rows, waiting for their orders. A few of the bigger girls, from the sixth form Owen guessed, were going around with clipboards, getting girls into their places.

Judging by their uniform, the Khedivial was not the only school represented. Girls – and they were all girls, for there were no boys among them – had come from all over Cairo. There were juniors as well as seniors. He even saw little Minya standing stoutly beside a bigger girl, who was holding her firmly by the hand. Owen guessed that that side of it had been as efficiently catered for as everything else.

A suffragi came out, saluted, and said: 'A telephone call for you, Effendi!'

Owen went inside to take it. It was his friend Paul, the Consul-General's ADC.

'What the hell is going on?' said Paul.

'They're demonstrating.'

'About what?'

'Marie Kewfik.'

'Can't you tell them to – well, go somewhere else?'

'No,' said Owen.

'Oh!'

There was a pause and then Paul said: 'Could you hold on, please.'

After a moment he returned.

'The Old Man says he's going to come down and address them personally.'

'That's what they want!'

'That's what they want?' asked Paul incredulously.

'The idea is to bring Marie to the attention of the Consul-General and the Khedive, and the Sirdar, and the Commander-in-Chief,' said Owen. 'But let's keep the Sirdar out of this.'

'I'll tell him to hold himself in readiness.'

'Tell him to hold himself far back,' said Owen. 'Out of the way.'

'I will. You realise, Gareth, that the army is itching to get its hands on the situation?'

'I'm sure. And, actually, Paul, I do feel tempted. To see what happens when the army is confronted by the Khedivial girls. Six-love, six-love, to the girls is my prediction.'

'I'll see if I can get some fool of an army officer to put money down on it. A lot of money. Then we can both retire in peace. However, I'm more worried about the Khedive. He's not used to this sort of thing. He doesn't believe in insurrection of any kind. Much less by women.'

'Schoolgirls first, harem ladies next, you mean?'

'That'll be the day!'

*   *   *

In the forecourt of the Bab-el-Khalk something was happening. The girls were preparing to move off. They marched out of the midan in orderly rows – 'A credit to their teachers,' said Paul, who had been unable to resist going down to see what was happening – and filed down the Sharia Ghane-el-Edaa towards the Midan Abdin and the Royal Palace.

Police were waiting for them, together with a harassed and anxious-looking Bimbashi McPhee, determined that there should be order, not so much on the girls' part as on the part of the police and the onlookers, who were also swelling in numbers. The Consul-General had not yet appeared. Paul had in any case re-routed his schedule to take him out to the leafy spaces of the Garden City of Kasr-el-Aini, where he would be greeted by the smiling faces of hordes of Wolf Cubs. At the direct request of the Government in Whitehall a new institution had been set up in Egypt, the Boy Scouts, to the bewilderment of the country in general and the tribes of Fuzzy Wuzzies, for whom tracking and living rough was the real thing. McPhee welcomed the new institution: Owen was among the rank of the bewildered.

The army was kept firmly out of the way, although a message came from the Sirdar to the effect that reinforcements were ready should McPhee need them. McPhee, who had enough trouble on his hands already, did not. At Owen's request, he softened his reply to say that he was greatly reassured that the army was standing by and that he would certainly call on them should the girls get out of hand.

While they were congregating in front of the Palace an old acquaintance came out to ogle the more nubile part of the maidenhood: Ali Osman.

'I say, Owen, they *are* developing nicely!'

'It's the heat,' said Owen.

And it mostly was, for as the sun rose higher and in the unshaded midan the temperature rose, some of the girls began surreptitiously to arrange their garments to give extra coolness. In doing so they couldn't help exposing their arms and other indecent parts of the body. There was a collective sigh from the soldiery, who had somehow moved forward, despite the best effort of their officers. The girls, recognising this and relishing the opportunities it provided for provocation, stepped up their efforts, until Layla and her fellow sixth-form leaders, in fury at this distraction from the main purpose of the exercise, began to move through the ranks twisting arms.

The situation was saved by the sudden appearance of the Consul-General, who, guessing what Paul was up to, had overruled his programming and insisted on coming to the demonstration. Having got there, however, and perhaps looking at his adversaries for the first time, he wavered. The regimental sergeant major, however, knew exactly what to do and called the parade to attention. This gave the cue to the Consul-General, who saluted. This, in turn, gave the quick-witted Paul the space he needed. He bent forward and breathed in the Consul-General's ear. The Consul-General thanked the girls for the concern they had shown, praised them for their efforts, and said that with their example before them, the Government would redouble its efforts to find the missing Marie. He thanked them again and said how much he admired them. Then saluted again. The RSM dismissed the parade. Everyone began to drift away. The girls were left standing there rather at a loss. Eventually, they, too, began to drift away.

Paul went up to the simmering Layla.

'Well done!' he said.

'Nothing's been done!' she said crossly.

'Oh, it has. He won't forget this in a hurry and tomorrow morning when he gets in, he'll find action notes which I have drafted and put on his desk.'

'And will they lead to action?'

'Oh, yes. If for no other reason than that a day or two later he'll find more notes on his desk asking for information about the action taken.'

'That's the way you do things, is it?'

'Yes. And when I'm doing it, it usually works.'

'People get moving, do they?'

'Yes. Of course, this doesn't guarantee that the action they take is the right action.'

'And do your notes go to the Mamur Zapt?'

'They do, yes.'

'And does he pay any attention to them?'

'That is an entirely different matter,' said Paul.

SEVEN

Layla walked slowly back from the Abdin Palace disregarding the efforts of her friends to engage her in conversation. She felt cheated. It had not turned out the way she had wanted it to. Perhaps she had expected too much for this was far, far short of what she had anticipated. She understood what that nice man, that friend of Owen's, had said, but he was just trying to be kind. The fact was that she'd not got anywhere. She had cocked it up. She wouldn't be able to try anything like this again. They'd never listen to her again, not after this. She was a silly little girl, desperate to do something that would help Marie, but not quite knowing what to do, and not doing it right.

Despite herself, the tears welled up in her eyes.

And then she knew what to do.

The awnings of the bazaars were ablaze with colour. Festoons of gaily striped blankets, white shawls, tasselled prayer carpets and embroidered saddlebags hung down from overhead. Vendors were walking about with strings of bright yellow shoes hung all over them like necklaces. The carpet-covered dikkas, or benches, outside the box-like shops, had picturesque statues of men sprawled on them, or sitting up with their hands around their knees. Powerful whiffs of scent came from just across the bazaar where the black, spider-like figures of the scentmakers sat.

Layla dodged between two narrow lines of boarded up shops and turned up a lane which appeared to have nothing in it. At the end was a stretch of blank hoarding draped with worn shawls and rugs.

'Greetings, daughter!' said the Old Woman of the souk.

'Greetings, mother!' said Layla, slipping into a space beside her and squatting down.

'What is it? You come to me with trouble.'

'Oh, it's nothing,' said Layla.

'Tears are never nothing,' said the Old Woman.

'I was just stupid, that's all.'

'Is it the parade?' said the Old Woman. 'What I saw was a brave parade. Is that stupid?'

'I expected it to work miracles,' said Layla.

'And perhaps it did,' said the Old Woman. 'Only sometimes they take time to work.'

'I think that's what the Englishman was saying.'

'What Englishman was this? The Mamur Zapt?'

'His friend.'

'Oh, worth listening to, then. What did he say?'

'He said that it was a beginning. And that he would follow it up by putting bits of paper on desks.'

'Yes,' said the Old Woman. 'That's the way it's done.'

'It seems footling to me,' said Layla.

'And perhaps it is,' agreed the Old Woman. 'But it's the way things are done these days. Not here in the souk but in the offices. And that is where the power is. Not in the souk. It's not in the souk.'

'That, too, is what I think the Englishman was saying. But it seems so far away! I feel so impotent!'

The Old Woman laughed.

'Don't we all,' she said. 'I daresay the Pasha feels that too. The Pasha in his palace, and the poor man at his gate. Rich man, poor man. Clever man, stupid. We all feel it. Women especially. As you are finding out. And that is a good thing – not that you should feel unimportant, but that you should find out. And perhaps the young will find it out first. And girls before boys? Your bright friends at the Khedivial?'

'It doesn't feel like that,' said Layla. 'A lot of them seem pretty stupid to me.'

'And perhaps they are. But some of them won't be. And they are the ones you'll have to work with.'

'There are not enough.'

'The number will grow. And you have made a start with your parade.'

'A washout!' said Layla. 'A complete washout!'

'A beginning,' said the Old Woman. 'Think of it as that. You have opened people's eyes. Is that bad?'

'They'll close them again,' said Layla.

'Then you'll just have to work to keep them open,' said the Old Woman.

A little later that morning Georgiades came ambling into the bazaar. He went into a scentmaker's shop and put something down on the dikka.

'Seen this before?' he asked.

'Looks like a stone,' said the scentmaker.

'It is a stone.'

'I've seen stones before,' said the scentmaker.

'I was just wondering if you'd seen this one.'

'Why should I have seen this one?'

'It was one of the stones thrown the other day in the souk, at your shop.'

'Little devils! Might have brained me.'

'Big devils,' said Georgiades. 'It wasn't little boys who did this, it was grown men. And what I was wondering was why should grown men throw stones at honest, decent shopkeepers?'

'You tell me!'

'If it was the British, and they were throwing stones at them, I could understand it. But why at ordinary Egyptians?'

'Have you some special reason for asking?'

'Yes. My wife was in the souk the other day, coming to your shop, as it happens. Only she didn't get there. She saw what was happening and said to herself, "That's not for me!" and turned round and went home. And when I got in, she sent me. "This is man's work," she said. And when I said: "Men's work? Buying scent?" she produced that stone. It wasn't a man who gave it me, it was my wife. "See this?" she said. "It's what was thrown at me. Or nearly thrown. It could have brained me!" And it would have. It's a big stone. "So you go," she said. "I'll go tomorrow," I said, thinking that by then things would have died down. "Yes, but I want it now," she said. "It's a present for Miriam. She's got a new baby." "Well, good for her," I said. "But I'll go tomorrow," and I did. That's when I came to see you. Only I didn't like to say who had made me come, because it sounds a bit silly. So I made up some story. But since then I've been thinking about it, and then I thought I'd come round to see you; you're a wise, experienced man.'

'I am, yes. But it still wouldn't have stopped me having my brains knocked out. Young devils!' said the shopkeeper.

'Old devils,' said the Greek. 'They were *old* devils.'

'Old devils,' corrected the shopkeeper.

'And what I want to know is: how does it come about that grown-up men are throwing stones in the souk and nearly hitting my wife! I thought I'd come and ask you, you being a knowledgeable man, and having an interest, as they say, in *not* having our brains knocked out.'

'God be praised, they weren't.'

'Quite so. But if it goes on like this, one day they will.'

'It's getting closer all the time, I can feel it.'

'And my wife, too, an innocent bystander!'

'I blame the government.'

'And the British.'

'They are the government.'

'Some say it was the gangs. I was talking to people in the Tentmakers' Bazaar, and they reckoned it was lads from the Kewfik stables who started it.'

'Well, it was. I recognised some of them. They come in regularly.'

'For scent?'

'No, no. I make up other things as well.'

'Like what?'

'Poison.'

'Poison? You never do!'

'I do. Not often of course. But sometimes the odd person requests it.'

'What do they want poison for?'

'To get rid of someone, I suppose. I never ask.'

'But – but – You said it was Kewfik boys who were asking?'

'That's right.'

'But – but – this is terrible! What do they want it for? Are they thinking of trying to kill off the Kauris?

'They'd need more than I gave them to do that.'

'Then . . .?'

'More likely their old man.'

'Old Kewfik?'

'He's not very popular around here.'

'Yes, but – and to get rid of him? Just like that?'

'There's plenty of people who'd be only too glad.'

'This is terrible!'

'It's a terrible world we live in, friend. But, look, don't take on so! Maybe they just want to put down the rats.'

'Rats?'

'There are sure to be rats in the stables.'

'I hadn't thought of that!'

'Well, you might not. You're a nice chap.'

'Yes, that must be it. I wouldn't like to think of it as intended for – well, you know: someone. Even old Kewfik.'

'Well, they wouldn't have needed it for him. He's half dead, anyway.'

'Perhaps that's why he's half dead! Someone's had a go at him already!'

'They said it was a heart attack. You know, over that girl of his. The one who was kidnapped.'

'That's true. And it might not be old Kewfik that it was aimed at, anyway.'

'It might have been the daughter.'

'What!'

'The daughter. Young love. You know, broken heart and all that. That boy she was so keen on, and then he went away. Why was that? A lover's tiff? A quarrel? And maybe he thought it was her fault and wanted revenge.'

'So he tried to poison her?'

'Young love, you know. Desperate for her. And then she turns him down. Walks out on him. He's a man of pride, and he's not having that. So he gets one of his mates in the stable yard – his father works there, doesn't he? – to get him some poison. And then, abracadabra it's done!'

'But it wasn't like that? I mean, it's *not* been done. She's been kidnapped!'

'Just in time, I would say.'

'What a mind you have,' said Georgiades admiringly.

'It's the scent,' said the scentmaker modestly. 'The fumes. They put ideas in your head.'

'They don't put ideas like that in *my* head. Although, now I come to think of it, I've had a funny feeling in my tummy lately. Do you think that could be something to do with it?'

'No. My products are all guaranteed to do the job they're meant for. And no other. If someone asks for fine-smelling scent, that's what they get. Poison – well, if that's what you want, what you especially ask for – that's what you get. And what you do with it afterwards is your concern not mine.'

'It could be rats.'

'Could be. Usually is. I don't get many people in here trying to poison the souk.'

'But you could. It's a bit like rats, isn't it?'

'Rats?'

'They say, wherever you are, you're never more than a yard away from a rat. Maybe it's like that with poison. Wherever you are, you're never more than a yard away from being poisoned.'

'Well, yes, but . . .'

'Just speculating. I mean, it could be, couldn't it?'

'Look, I don't think it's very likely.'

'No, no, of course not. But I do get tummy ache occasionally . . .'

'I can give you something for that.'

'I'm not sure . . .'

'You'll be as right as rain in a day or two.'

'But it never rains here!'

'I don't think so,' said Owen dismissively.

'Nor do I really,' said Georgiades. 'But they were trying to buy poison.'

'Forget about the poison. Go and call on the Kauri boys. There's some sort of warfare going on around the Kewfik stables and we need to know what it's about.'

Nikos was handling the ransom negotiations, as no one else in the department, including Owen, had a clue what numbers were all about. He didn't like it, mainly because it would probably mean stepping outside his office, which he never liked to do. He had a strong sense of territoriality. Within his usual four walls, he felt secure. If he stepped outside them, you never know what might happen. Girls, for instance, might come at you.

But there was no escaping this. Of all Owen's staff, Nikos had
the best financial brain. The only financial brain, Owen sometimes thought – and he didn't trust anybody, including himself.
Figures, to Nikos, were for checking. Again and again. People
thought he was peculiar. Including most ordinary Egyptians. The
thing was he was an ordinary Egyptian. Like most of them when
he went to an eating or smoking house, he liked to play dominoes.
This, ordinarily, was not very mathematical. But the way Nikos
played them *was* mathematical. As he played, he ran through
various mathematical possibilities. He had an incredible facility
for calculating odds. You might have thought that there wasn't
much scope for this when playing dominoes. But the Cairo
aficionados played to win and there was much betting on the
results. Between these games there was an intellectual brandishing
of theories, and considerable argument. What might issue from
using a particular configuration? From using one configuration
rather than another? You had to keep a lot of moves in your
mind, rather like chess.

Nikos was a chess player too. It was a way of structuring the
world, and Nikos liked to structure the world. In theory, that was.
Not in practice. For practical restructuring, Georgiades was your
man. Or Georgiades's wife, who was a financial wizard, and
played regularly on the Cairo Bourse, to Georgiades's terror.
Rosa, however, made a lot of money, which was just as well,
because Georgiades didn't. Rosa sometimes erected fear moun-
tains of what might happen should her children turn out like him
rather than like her. Nikos was of the Rosa school of high stakes,
although he usually lacked her capacity and willingness to back
her calculations by actually putting money down.

Contact had been made with the kidnappers' negotiators and
negotiations were proceeding. Nikos, terrified but suspicious, and
even more suspicious than he was terrified, which was probably
the right way round, knew what he was after: spinning out the
negotiations and not actually getting anywhere. Although getting
sufficiently somewhere to persuade the kidnappers that he was
serious and that the negotiations would issue in good things for
the kidnappers. Nikos could play this game out to eternity. Or
at least until there came a point when he realized what he had
just committed himself to and then his brain would seize up, at

which point Owen would take over. Owen knew nothing about numbers but he did know about power, and he had the priceless sense of knowing what he wanted from the numbers.

Cairo kidnappers were not mathematically sophisticated but they, too, knew what they wanted. Bring in the banks, who were usually financing ransom negotiations, and you had quite a strong team on the Owen side.

Owen hoped that this would stand them in good stead this time over the Marie negotiations. Provided, of course, that no one on the other side panicked.

Early on, part of the negotiations was for the kidnappers to prove that Marie was still alive and in their possession, in exchange for putting real money on the table. And this meant producing the real girl, or at any rate showing her. This was a sticking point for the kidnappers and at first they wouldn't play. They weren't producing anybody. But then that meant that Nikos would not produce anything either. It was the usual impasse. Nikos had been here before, many times, and knew what to do and what would resolve the impasse: money, naturally. But how much? And under what conditions?

Owen would be standing by when the kidnappers showed Marie, in case there was an opportunity to snatch her, but, of course, the kidnappers were very probably also experienced and would also be planning to foil any attempt to do that. So, Nikos mused, he must plan for all possibilities but move one step at a time.

The first step was to talk to the bank so that Nikos would have real money to lay on the table at the very start of negotiations. Real money would persuade the kidnappers as nothing else would. It would not be enough, of course, not even to convince as a preliminary offer. Nikos would have to raise it, which he was quite prepared to do as an indication of seriousness. But little by little, step by step, the kidnappers would have to produce Marie each time, as an indication of their seriousness. And so it would progress. Or not progress.

A message came from Marie's aunt, the Khedive's wife: *What is happening? And why isn't it happening faster?*

It all took time, Owen patiently explained. And that required patience. She must be patient.

And meanwhile, said the Khedive's wife, *the poor child might be killed!*

That was true, Owen admitted; but it was a risk that had to be run.

Back came another message: *Would a little more money help?*

Probably; but Owen did not want to play this card yet.

The Khedive's wife hoped he knew what he was doing.

Owen hoped so too – and did not send a message back.

Then came another message: *Marie's mother is collapsing.*

Give her support, was Owen's reply.

Next message (from the Khedive's wife): *You are going to need support if this goes wrong!* (Confidential message via McPhee).

(Of course, the other side would be twitching too.)

End of messages for the time being.

Meanwhile discussions were proceeding. Nikos thought he was beginning to get somewhere.

There was a lull.

Nikos thought it might be the time to increase the stakes a little, he put more money on the table.

Then there was another lull, and then a reply from the kidnappers, demanding still more.

Nikos required another production of Marie. This was initially refused. But eventually, reluctantly, Marie was produced. She seemed unharmed.

Now Nikos switched to discussing how the final handover of the cash, on the one side, and Marie, on the other, might be handled. This was always an important part of the discussions, because it kept the kidnappers involved and optimistic. Marie could not be harmed while this was going on. At the same time the kidnappers would be getting used to the discussions, gaining confidence, even trusting Nikos, since he appeared to be negotiating in good faith and to be willing ultimately to disburse the money. As a guarantee of this he produced some bags of coin and bundles of notes; then took them away again.

In the last resort, the deal would be a genuine one. There was always the strength of Owen's side. In the last resort, the money was there and it would be produced if Marie was produced. Their priority was to rescue Marie.

'We can always get the kidnappers another time,' said Owen.

Layla came to see him.

How were things going, she wanted to know.

He didn't mind seeing her; first, because he liked her, and thought she deserved it. Second, because, who knows, he might be able to make use of her at some stage. She hung around, twisting her fingers.

'Would it help,' she asked, 'if we were to offer an exchange?'

'We are offering money,' he said. 'That's what it is all about.'

'I wasn't thinking of that,' said Layla. 'I was thinking of me.'

'You?' he said, surprised.

'Yes. If I swapped places with Marie, pending the outcome of the negotiations?'

'What would be the point of that?'

'You could say that the strain was telling on Marie's family and you were afraid her mother might die.'

'That would only make them think they were getting somewhere. That we would have to give in soon.'

'The strain might be telling on Marie, too. You could say that if they didn't watch out, they might kill the goose that was laying the golden egg.'

Owen shook his head.

'That would be open to the same objection. If they really thought that, they might think that they were soon going to be able to close the deal.'

'I just want to help.'

'I know. But I don't want to lose you as well as Marie. And we have to think of your parents too.'

'They're pretty tough . . .'

'Yes, but I'm not. I know you want to help, and maybe there'll be something you can do later. But not this.'

'It's just that nothing seems to be happening.'

'But it is. And part of this is waiting for the other side to crumble.'

'I suppose this is the way it has to be in negotiations?'

'It is. And especially when someone's life is at stake. None of us likes it.'

As she went out, he said: 'If I can see a place for you later, I won't forget.'

Nikos was conducting his operations from a small room in the Khan-el-Kalil, a corner of the great mosque area. It had belonged to one of the banks and was used by them as a poor man's counting house – a place where poorer Egyptians went to settle their debts. There wasn't much to it. It consisted really of a single room with a counter. Customers would come in and wait for their turn to be summoned to the counter. They sat on the floor with their back against the walls and went up to the counter when their names were called. They would sometimes wait for hours and the walls were grimy with the dirt from their turbans. At the counter, the coins would be placed on the surface and be literally counted by the two clerks. Then they would be put in a bag and either taken behind the counter to an office to be stored for a time before being passed on or else put down under the counter on to the floor to await collection, which would not be long.

The sums dealt in were never large – the paper bags put on the floor contained a shop's takings for the morning – and most of the money was paid out by hand. It was rumoured that the counting house was actually part of a larger bank which did not like to acknowledge this lesser side of its operations. Some people would never go to a big bank, they were put off by its impersonality and sheer size. They had always gone to a counting house and continued to do so. It had the confidence of its customers. Which was why it had been chosen as the operational site of the present transaction. All transactions took place in hard coin. Even grubby notes were suspect. This made settling difficult for a bank that had the job of finding the necessary coin if the sum was large, as it would be in this case.

The room was small, dirty and dark. There was also an inner room into which people would go to hand over big transactions. It was probably a sign of confidence that the kidnappers had agreed to it. Nevertheless, it was equally possible that it was an indication of the unreality of their dreams.

With so many of the ordinary poor in it, the room smelled strongly of garlic. There was no window and not much circulation of air. The room, like so many in Cairo, was underground

and therefore – although this was aspiration rather than reality
– cooler. Nikos drowned himself in eau de cologne before going
in, which assisted negotiations because it convinced the clientele
of the impossible richness of the man with the money.

Nikos stayed in the smaller interior room throughout.

At some point in the morning, three women appeared dressed
in burkas and long veils. Two of them were actually not women;
the third was Marie.

A little later two more burka-clad figures went in. These *were*
actually women. One of them was Layla, whose job it was to
see that it really was Marie who was produced. Owen had
thought a lot about this. He needed someone who could identify
Marie. Her mother was too distraught to be able to manage this
and he had considered a maid from the household. On further
consideration, however, Layla would do it equally well, if not
better. She knew Marie, of course and, Owen thought, could
be guaranteed not to get in a flutter. Besides, it would make up
for his rejection of her earlier offer.

He went with her himself to the counting house where the
inspection would take place, although he would not go in. Inside,
Nikos would have a knife and a gun. Like all Owen's men he
knew how to use them. As a further precaution Owen insisted
on the kidnappers being searched before allowing Layla to be
taken into the room. They seemed inclined to demur but Owen
insisted. Two further men joined the kidnappers' side but did not
go into the inner room.

All this, thought Owen, and it was only an issue of a small
portion of the exchanging money that was at stake. When the
final exchange took place, of course, the money put down would
be much larger.

He met Layla beforehand in the Bab-el-Khalk. He thought
hard about this too, but decided it would put the seal of authority
on the proceedings.

She would go to the counting house in the company of two
burly women. Owen did not have any female police constables
but he did have burly women in plenty. They, like Layla, were
given careful instructions. One of them, Fatima, was Selim's wife
and huge, like him, a match, Owen considered, for any two
normal men. She had been instructed by Selim to lay down her

life if necessary to prevent any harm coming to Layla, and, probably, Marie. She needed no instruction, though. She and Selim were childless and children for them were sacrosanct.

Owen said goodbye to Layla in the Bab-el-Khalk.

'I won't let you down,' she promised, a little tearfully.

'And I won't let you down,' he said. 'All you have to do is give a shout.'

A feature of the smaller room in the counting house was that there was a concealed observation window, installed by the bank for the protection of its staff. The interview with the kidnappers would be observed the whole time. There was also a door through which Owen's men could burst in an instant if it was required.

Owen himself occupied the observation room. He took an experienced, intelligent sergeant with him. With the two of them, the small room was stifling.

He watched Nikos come in, then two men who he guessed were the kidnappers. One of them, it soon became apparent, had skills at counting. Owen made a note of him. Later, perhaps, they would pick him up.

The kidnappers were nervous. If Nikos was, he did not show it.

He produced two bags of coins and opened them on the table in front of the kidnappers, and then spread the coins before him. The men watched, spellbound.

'Count,' he instructed.

The man the kidnappers had chosen as their counter ran expertly through the pile of coin. When he had finished, he nodded and the other kidnapper went to the door and signified that they could proceed.

The three burka-clad figures had been sitting in the outer room, their backs against the wall. On the signal from the kidnappers inside, they passed into the counting room.

Almost at once, Layla appeared with Selim's wife. The third of their party waited outside.

The identification was done in a flash. Marie removed her veil and Layla removed hers – although that was not part of Owen's explicit instructions. The two girls stared at each other, both of them fighting back tears.

Nikos nodded and Layla and Selim's wife were shown out.

As they had both instructed, they did not say anything to each other and proceeded to the Bab-el-Khalk.

A moment later Marie left, accompanied by her guards. They disappeared into the souk. Although Owen had watchers, they lost sight of them.

However, they now knew Marie was still alive. This was the main thing. Owen took encouragement, too, from the fact that everything had proceeded as they had arranged. That suggested that later, more complex arrangements could work too.

All was proceeding as planned.

EIGHT

S elim was agitated. He had been agitated all morning, ever
since Fatima had gone off. Could they be trusted to get it
right? Even Fatima?

Eventually he could bear it no longer and went along to the
Bab-el-Khalk. At the office they said that Owen was still out,
and so was Nikos. What part Nikos had to play in all this, Selim
was not sure. He had never quite been able to make Nikos out.
He was different from everybody else at the police station. He
stayed in his room and rarely went out. What he did in there all
the time Selim couldn't see. Something to do with paper. He
always had papers in his hand and was always peering at them.
Selim never peered at papers. His mind went into a fog at once
whenever they were presented to him. Some people were born
to play with papers, others not. Selim was definitely not. He had
never been able to get on with Nikos, but knew that everyone
thought he was very clever and that the boss trusted him, which
was enough for Selim. Still, even demi-gods could slip up. And
they had been gone a long time.

He wandered out on to the street and back to his usual spot.
It was early in the morning and the children were on their way
to school. He looked out for Minya. He always did these days.
He looked forward to seeing her happy little face, her cheerful
little skips. If he had had a little girl he would have liked her to
be like this. He had never been able to understand people who
were unkind to children and it disturbed him. Lately he had fallen
into the habit of going each day along the route on which he
knew he would meet her. Often he gave her a sweet. Ever since
he had seen her eyes light up at the scentmaker's shop, he had
got into the habit of popping into the shop and buying a boiled
sweet for her. He had one in his pocket now.

Ah, there she was! She had been looking out for him too, as
she did every day now. It wasn't just the sweet, she had got used
to this big shambling man whom the Mamur Zapt, no less, had

told to protect her. She knew he would. She could just feel it. She didn't mind not going without Marie now, although she still thought about her a lot, and when she did would clutch hard at Selim's great hand.

This morning she was singing a little song to herself. It was one that Selim knew too, one that he remembered from his own childhood, and oftentimes he joined in, although he never sang it quite right. Sometimes she tried to correct him, although his voice would never go quite where it ought. It was, however, a comforting voice to have beside you as you went to school. Since Marie had disappeared, there had been other girls assigned to accompany her but after a while, recognising their redundancy while Selim was around, they had dropped out. Selim never dropped out. She had told her mother about him and how the Mamur Zapt had told him to look after her and her mother sometimes looked out for them both and gave Selim a cake, one of those sticky ones from the man at the corner.

Things were going well for Minya this morning and she opened her mouth and sang out loud. Beside her, Selim joined in, in a low rumble and, hearing the two of them, sometimes other people joined in too. This morning everyone was singing.

The Old Woman of the souk came out and listened and told her she was like a little bird. The Old Woman was talking to a lady this morning dressed in a long black dress, like a burka but not a burka. After a moment, this lady joined in too. She had a really lovely voice which thrilled Minya to the core. The lady was singing a song Minya thought she knew, but she didn't quite, and when the lady stopped, she asked her what the song was. The lady said she didn't know its title, she had learned it when she was very small, about Minya's size, but she thought it was very beautiful. The Old Woman knew it too, and even tried to join in, but her voice was wavering and quavering and after a short while she stopped and said she couldn't manage it these days. But the scentmaker came out of his shop and said that hearing such singing made his heart rejoice.

Aisha, Mahmoud's wife, on her way to school with her two small children, stopped for a moment to listen. It gave her an idea and that afternoon, when Mahmoud got back from his office, she suggested they go out for the evening. They hadn't done that for some time but before the children had arrived they had gone out often, usually to a small club where they would dine and dance and listen to the music.

Mahmoud lit up.

'Yes,' he said, 'before we get too old!'

They discussed where they should go.

The deciding factor was the music. Both of them were very fond of music but they had a very definite taste. Despite being a modern, Europeanised couple, and following French taste in many things, when it came to music they preferred the old classical style with its roots in traditional Arab music. Not the belly-wobbling style preferred by tourists and, these days, increasingly by working men, but the old music with its roots in folk song. But it had to be genuine and good. They both knew enough about it to shrink from the false folky rhythms that were springing up nowadays. The scene, though, would probably have changed since the days when they used to go out regularly. They wanted good players and a good awalim.

And then Mahmoud remembered the Serpent of the Nile and what Owen had said about its awalim there.

'Let's go to the Serpent,' he said.

'Will it still be there?'

'Oh, yes,' said Mahmoud. 'Gareth said he'd been there very recently and the awalim was good.'

Aisha looked at him suspiciously.

'Is this work or pleasure?' she said.

'Pleasure,' said Mahmoud firmly. Honesty compelled him to add, 'Although, we might see that boy there.'

'What boy?'

'The one who was going around with that Kewfik girl. Shawquat, his name is. Apparently he is a promising *nay* player. Although he probably won't be playing tonight.'

'All right,' said Aisha. 'If it's a case of doing something for that poor girl, I don't mind.'

It was still early in the evening when they arrived and the place was only about two-thirds full. No singer was in evidence and even the main musicians had not yet arrived. There was just a *kamanjah* and a *kanoon*. The *kamanjah* was a kind of viol and the *kanoon* a dulcimer. They were often used as a low-key accompaniment to a singer. As soon as Aisha heard them, she knew that they had come to the right place. In the true old Arab music the tones were divided into thirds, which gave a distinctive softness and subtlety to the sound. Her Egyptian musical friends claimed that European music was deficient in the number of sounds it could produce. Certainly Aisha sometimes felt that Arab music was smoother and more subtle.

They were still on their eggplants and quail when the awalim came in.

The tall, black, imposing figure strode to the platform. The musicians, augmented now from the *kamanjah* and *kanoon*, sat at her feet. Aisha suddenly realised that the now-crowded room had fallen still.

And then the awalim began.

She sang first a very old, very simple song, a song which you might have heard in the nursery, and probably many of her hearers had. Then it modulated into an old, gentle love song, and then another, and then another. The music wasn't like Western music. Her singing was part of the orchestral ensemble; it wasn't being accompanied by the orchestra, it was integral to it. As it warmed up it seemed to flow, to become liquid. It poured around its hearers, until they too were part of the music, blended into it. The audience was absolutely quiet. Several of them were crying. Aisha felt herself crying too. The music seemed to reach right into the listeners, to go deeper and deeper until it touched the very roots.

And then suddenly it stopped. No one seemed to be breathing, although several people murmured quietly, almost to themselves. And then, of course, the awalim broke off, bowed and stalked out. Behind her the room exploded.

Gradually the applause died down and was replaced by a continuing appreciative murmur. People talked quietly, touched each other.

Aisha became aware of a boy beside her, right at the front, next to the stage. He was weeping noiselessly. She wondered if it was the Shawquat boy.

Moved by a sudden instinct, Aisha leaned across and patted him on the shoulder. He looked round at her, startled, as if he was coming out of a deep sleep.

'Do you love her very much?' she asked compulsively.

'Yes!' he said passionately. 'More than—'

He broke off, and the tears flowed.

'Do you sing yourself? Or play?'

'Play.'

'What do you play?'

'The *nay*.'

And then another impulse rose in her, or perhaps it was a half memory.

'Did you play for Marie?'

Now the tears came irresistibly.

'Or with her?'

'How do you know about Marie?'

'We've all been following.'

'We?'

'I was at the Khedivial.'

'Marie's school?'

'Yes. Although not at the same time. A bit before her. But in my mind she is still a schoolmate.'

'Yes,' said the boy. 'Yes.'

Aisha placed her hand on his.

'She *will* be back. They will find her.'

He wept unrestrainedly.

'I let them take her away,' he said brokenly. 'I should have fought for her. As a man would have done.'

'They were many and you were one.'

'I shouldn't have let them take her.'

'There was nothing you could do.'

Of course others in the club could hear him crying. They looked at him, however, with nothing but sympathy. They didn't know what it was about but they could understand that he was distressed, and, with the ready Arab sympathy, felt moved for and with him.

Aisha decided to move him on.

'You are a *nay* player? I like the *nay*. I tried to play it myself, but I was hopeless.'

'It is not easy.'

'When did you start playing?'

'When I was three. My father didn't like it. He said: "It is not an instrument for a man." But my mother said: "He is not a man, he is a boy still, and a little one at that. And he has talent. You can hear it." "I just hear noise," my father said. "And so we should not listen to you," my mother said. They let me play. And some of my father's friends heard it and said: "The boy is good. And he will get better. And when he gets better, we will come and hear him." And that pleased my father and he said: "Well, well, perhaps we will let him play then. Only he has to do other things as well. There are things to be done in Egypt.""

'What did he mean?' asked Mahmoud.

'Oh, he didn't think music was real work. Not real men's work. And, besides . . .'

'Yes?'

'He wanted me to walk in his footsteps.'

'At the stables?'

'Yes. And not only in the stables. More broadly.'

'More broadly?'

'My father wanted to build another Egypt. A bigger, better Egypt. One free from the Pashas. And from the British. But I was not interested in these things. All I was interested in was music and my father said to my mother: "Look what he has turned into! This is no boy of mine!" "His aims are different from yours," my mother said, "that is all." But although she spoke for me, her heart was half with my father. They both wanted to build a better Egypt. She worked for that, as well as he, and they were both disappointed that I did not care as much as they did about big things. But actually, I do care about them. They are what I want to put into my music.'

There was a movement beside them. Someone had come to stand by them at the table. It was the awalim.

'Are you troubled, brother?' she said to the boy.

'I'm all right,' said the boy.

'He is with friends,' said Aisha.

'He carries a big trouble with him,' said Mahmoud.

'I know,' said the awalim.

'Your music will heal him,' said Aisha politely.

'It hasn't healed me,' said the awalim.

                         *   *   *

She went back on to the platform and resumed her singing. Only now she was not singing the same songs. Instead of the songs of lovers, they were songs of old heroes. The audience began to clap out the rhythm. Mahmoud and Aisha clapped with them; the boy listened, rapt.

'Was that what you wanted to do?' asked Aisha, in a pause. 'Make music like that?'

'Oh, yes,' whispered the boy. 'Yes.'

The awalim brushed past them on her way out.

'Was that the music you came to hear?' she asked. 'Or the other sort?'

'Both,' said Mahmoud. 'The good thing about music is that there is room for both, and more.'

'Well, you do ask for a lot from your evening out!' said the awalim.

The awalim bowed her head in acknowledgement.

The boy sat on, as if stunned.

Aisha leaned forward.

'Are you looking for work?'

'Work?' he said, as if waking from a deep sleep.

'I have three small children, and I would like the two eldest to have music lessons.'

'How old are they?'

'Four and three.'

'That is very young.'

'You told me that you yourself started at three.'

'Yes, but—'

Aisha laughed.

'I am not expecting you to turn them into playing like yourself. I simply want them—' she hesitated – 'to be touched by music, so that it will live inside them and grow inside them – perhaps this is not simple after all!'

'It is not. It is the most wonderful thing anyone can do. It is not work, it is – it is a privilege!' He stopped. 'But I don't think I can do it, I don't know how to. Music, yes, of course. I know about that. But teaching it is a different thing. Especially in ones so small . . .'

'I am sure you could manage it. They are not difficult children and I think they like music. They like it when I sing to them. They even like it when their father sings to them.'

'The less said about that the better,' said Mahmoud.

'I think it is in them. But how do you take them further? What is the next step? That I don't know.'

The boy was thinking.

'It may not be best to start with the *nay*. It is, as you say, a difficult instrument to learn. Perhaps I could bring along a *tabl* – a small drum, boys usually like that. And maybe a *sagat* – girls like that, it's like castanets, but, really boys like it as well. I will bring along a selection, and I will play my *nay* and they can accompany me. Yes! They would like that. And it builds up a sense of rhythm, which, of course, they will have naturally.'

'There!' said Aisha. 'You do know something about it! I'm sure you would be good at teaching. And they would love it.'

'I could try, couldn't I? I mean, I would like to try. It must be a wonderful thing to help children to start. It would be such a privilege to open out a world – yes. I would really love to do that.'

'Good. Then you can come round to our house and start tomorrow.'

'Yes!'

'Now, about money.'

'Oh, I wouldn't want any money! It is such a wonderful thing to do.'

'We must give you some money. It wouldn't be fair otherwise. Just a little. Not enough, I'm afraid, to make you rich.'

'I don't want to be rich! I just want to be happy in what I'm doing, and to make other people happy.'

'Well, that's very nice. All the same . . .'

'I suppose,' said the boy meditatively, 'I could save up and then the Kewfiks might look more favourably on me.'

'Look we weren't thinking of quite that amount of money!'

'No, no, of course not. But over time it would build up, and then perhaps they'd let us marry.'

'Perhaps. But don't bank on it,' said Mahmoud.

'You should certainly try!' said Aisha severely. 'How else are you going to get anywhere? I remember when Mahmoud and I got married he had no money at all.'

'And still haven't,' said Mahmoud.

One of the principal duties of the Mamur Zapt was to keep his eye on the Cairo gangs. They were different from the gangs in other places, in Chicago, say, or in Sicily, in that they were almost exclusively politically driven. Making money was a by-product but not their main point. That was where the Mamur Zapt came in. His was an essentially political appointment. Both the British and the Khedive saw his main function as the preserver of order. The British Army, as an army of occupation, saw that as their function too. This created a tension between the military authorities and the civil ones. In the eyes of the Consul-General, who administered Egypt on behalf of the English Government, the British Army was best kept out of it. They were too heavy-handed and as likely to cause trouble as to prevent it. That was the view of the Khedive, too. He disliked both authorities, the civil and the military: at a pinch though, he preferred the civil one. In his early years he had seen British soldiers marching through Cairo and didn't want to see that again. The British were there, he continually pointed out, only by virtue of treaty. And treaties were two-sided. His interpretation was that the British had come to Egypt by invitation; and politeness, if nothing else, required that they shouldn't throw their weight around too heavily.

This was where Owen came in. He was, in theory, an appointment of the Khedive and not of the British, and was therefore, in theory, answerable to him and not to them. It was a fiction that both sides, at different times, found convenient. He could be disowned by both. On the other hand, he could appeal to either, switching shelter as was convenient. You had to have a certain skill to operate with two masters. This skill Owen had in abundance.

The great fear of both the Khedive and the Consul-General was that the country would begin boiling over from below. It was the duty of the Mamur Zapt to prevent this. Owen sometimes wished that this part of his role had been explained to him before he took up the job.

But there he was, in the job, and so far, surviving. The art was never to let things get to a head. Which was why he watched developments in the souk or in the club so carefully. And particularly among the young. Egypt had a lot of young, and, like the young generally, they had a lot of volatility. So maybe what happened in the Scentmakers' Bazaar was worth paying attention to. And it was particularly worth paying attention to when they took on a Nationalist tinge.

And, sooner or later, they almost inevitably did. Stone throwing in the Scentmakers'? Kids' stuff. But when the kids became students it was no longer quite kids' stuff. And when the students became stablemen it was even harder.

In the confined space of the stables the heat was overwhelming. So was the smell. The horses were no longer in there but had left huge quantities of dung behind. The men had been sweeping it up and had shovelled it into a large pile. They were waiting for someone to come with the cart and then it could be taken away. In the meantime, they sat in the yard drinking the strong, bitter black tea of the Egyptian peasant. They offered some to Georgiades, which he accepted gratefully.

'Where's Abdullah?' someone asked. 'I was expecting him to come and tell us what to do next.'

'He's talking to Shawquat.'

At the mention of the name, Georgiades pricked up his ears.

'He's always talking to Shawquat!'

'I wish he would talk to Abdullah and talk some sense into him. We really ought to have a go at the Kauris. It's four now. That's no joke! We ought to go after them. Teach them a lesson. Otherwise they'll walk right over us!'

'Aren't they doing that now?'

'I don't know what's come over Abdullah. He used not to be like this!'

'He listens to Shawquat too much.'

'Why should he suddenly start listening to him? He never listens to me!'

'He thinks he has the ear of the mighty.'

'He's too ready to *listen* to the mighty. What good has it ever done him? Or us?'

'Ah, but it will some day.'

'Sure it will! But meanwhile four of our mates have got killed.'

'Wait, he says. Until we can all act together.'

'The Kauri boys aren't waiting, are they? No, instead, they're getting stuck into us!'

'Soon, he says, soon!'

'Oh, yes? And what is "soon"?'

'*Bokra*,' said someone. 'Tomorrow – if tomorrow ever comes!'

'Let's not hang about, let's get started ourselves.'

'We'd be on our own, Shawquat says. And then they'd wipe us out.'

'And, meanwhile, we *are* being wiped out! By the Kauri boys!'

'Shawquat says to wait until the others come in with us.'

'That's what the mighty tell him, is it? You know, if I had the ear of the mighty, as he says he does, I'd be tempted to spit into it!'

'The thing is, we're held up because of that girl.'

'What the hell has she got to do with it?'

'The Kauris think they can make some real money out of her.'

'Is any of that money likely to come to me?'

'No.'

'You can forget about that, then.'

'The Kauris would make a difference if they came in with us. There's a lot of them. Shawquat says it would be stupid to move without them.'

'Do you know what I think? I think the Kauris are more interested in the money than they are in Shawquat and his big plans!'

'He says it's only a question of waiting for a day or two.'

'He says!'

'It's very near, he says. On the brink. And then we can all get going. Together. And that'll give us a better chance of success than if we do it on our own.'

'Us and the Kauris? Working together? I'll believe it when I see it! Look, I think we're wasting time. Let's get on with it.'

'Give them a couple of days.'

'They'll want more.'

'Tell Shawquat to tell them they can't have more.'

'Unless they cut us in.'

There was a silence.

'That's an idea,' someone said.

'It is.'

There was a general murmur of assent.

'Tell Shawquat to talk about that!' said a new voice.

Owen, meanwhile, was sauntering through the Ezbekiya Gardens. It was afternoon and the only other people there were nursemaids with their charges. They were gathering round the bandstand, where a band was beginning to warm up. It was an Egyptian band which blew and blasted, not quite in the manner that the fastidious Mahmoud and Aisha would have liked but in a jolly way which appealed to the children clustered around.

A little later, the music would take a different turn, as would the gardens. Blinds would be pulled back on the upper floor of the buildings which surrounded the gardens, to reveal bulky ladies who leaned out of the windows and dangled scarves to attract the attention of passers-by. The passers-by were usually, at this later hour, British soldiers who frequented the squalid bars on the ground floors of the buildings. To provide for them there was a different kind of music. Much of the music was provided by the soldiers themselves. They played old favourites of the English music halls, sometimes on battered pianos, sometimes on instruments the soldiers had brought themselves. It was a favourite place for off-duty soldiers to gather over beer.

There was also – a great attraction – an all-female band. A European band, which deepened the attraction even more. The girls were reported to be either white slaves or freed white slaves, and they brought to their listeners the sounds of home. Not always English homes. Mixed in were the sounds of the Estaminets and also the sounds of the popular cafes of Rumania and Russia and unknown countries of central Europe. The music could be best described as a lively mix. Again, it was not music of the sort to appeal to Mahmoud or Aisha, whose French-based tastes were more sophisticated and, anyway, included the more traditional native Egyptian songs.

Owen stopped near the all-girl band.

'Hello, darling,' they chirruped cheerfully.

He waved back.

'Not today, darlings!'

'Oh!' they wailed in pretend disappointment.

'There's something I wanted to ask you.'

'Any time! Here, or upstairs?'

'I wouldn't want to encourage pure maidens like you to give way to temptation.'

'Oh, that's a pity!'

'What was the question you wanted to ask? It doesn't sound very interesting.'

'It's to do with that girl who was kidnapped.'

The girls in the Ezbekiya knew all the gossip of Cairo; and about girls who disappeared.

'Lucky her!' someone sighed.

'Not so lucky, I suspect. I want to find her.'

'She wasn't one of us?'

'No. But she was interested in music.'

This caught their attention.

'She had a boyfriend who played the *nay*.'

'Not our style, darling!'

'I know. But they used to hang about in music venues. I thought there might be a chance that you had come across them.'

'Give us more information.'

Owen described Marie and young Shawquat.

'We'll keep our eyes open for them,' they promised.

'Is there money in it?' someone asked.

'There could be. But the main thing is that she is a nice girl and I don't want harm to come to her.'

'We'll look out for her. But if she has been kidnapped, we wouldn't see her, would we? They'll have her locked up.'

'The thing is that I think some of the men who kidnapped her might be interested in music too. They had picked out the boy when he was still at school.'

'Like that, were they?'

'No. Not necessarily. I have no reason to think they were. I think the pair were genuinely interested in music.'

'Where did they hang around?'

'In the Geziret. It's not far from here. And you know the music connection . . .'

'We need more to go on.'

'I'll try and find it. Just keep your ears open, will you? I think these people will be the sort who would talk.'

'Do they play? Musicians who play, often do. It goes with the drink.'

'Is she talking about us?' a fresh voice asked.

There was a general laugh.

'Surely not!' said Owen. 'But the Ezbekiya is a place where people gather. And someone might say something.'

'If they do, we'll let you know.'

'It's the girl,' said Owen. 'That is why I came to you. I thought you might be inclined to help.'

'We are, love, we are!' they assured him. 'But I don't think it'll help much.'

Coming out of the Gare Centrale, on his way into the Geziret, Mahmoud was nearly knocked over by an arabeah rushing to deposit its passengers. It reminded him of that earlier occasion when the child had been knocked over and he had picked the child up and taken it home to its mother. That was not far from here. He was on his way now to follow up the stabbing of the Kewfik stableman, and since that meant visiting the Kauri boys, he had arranged to join up with Owen, who would be coming from the Ezbekiya.

As he was going through the Geziret a woman dashed out of one of the houses and gave him a pastry she'd warmed from her oven. He recognised her. It was the woman whose child he had picked up. In the Geziret you didn't forget things like that. He thanked her courteously – Mahmoud was always courteous – and asked how the child was. The mother replied that he was getting better every day. Mahmoud gave thanks to Allah and asked her if she would join him in eating the pastry while it was still warm. They squatted down by the communal tap to eat it.

She asked him what he was doing in these parts and when he told her that he was following up a case of a stabbing, she nodded her head.

'Yes,' she said, 'that would be Hamid. He worked at the Kewfiks' stables, which are nearby, and there had been a quarrel between him and one of the Kauri boys, who also worked nearby.'

Mahmoud said that it was a pity that such quarrels had to end in a death and the woman agreed, but said that it had always been so in the Geziret. It had been so in her father's time and in her father's father's. But this killing of Hamid was bad because there had been no real reason for it. There had, indeed, recently been talk of peace, of the two sides, the Kauris and the Kewfik stablemen, coming together. And many in the Geziret had rejoiced. But some had not and had spoken bitterly against it. And a group of them had been speaking like that when Hamid had chanced to walk by.

And someone had said: 'There is a Kewfik man! Let us kill him and that will put a stop to all talk of peace between us.' And someone else had said: 'Let it be so!' And so they killed Hamid. But, afterwards, others said that it was wrong to kill a man like that, to brush him aside as if he had been a fly, when all he had been doing was walking by.

And there had been much dispute in the Geziret about it, with some taking one side and others the other. But Hamid's wife had raised her voice and demanded justice. And her sisters had supported her and called on her brothers to avenge Hamid. But others had said: 'Let us not fight over this.' The Geziret seemed to be tearing itself apart, with men raising their hands against their brother. And the women had spoken angrily about it and said that the elders should not allow such foolishness to happen. And the elders had been taken aback that the women should raise their voices. And some had suggested that the views of a wise man should be sought.

But Hamid's wife had said that it was because they had been listening to the views of men who thought they were wise and were not that such a terrible event had come to pass, and that they would do better to listen to the views of some wise women. And someone had suggested the Old Woman of the souk . . .

NINE

Selim's patrols now regularly took in the Khedivial Girls'
School. This had not been part of Owen's assignment and
Selim was uneasy about how far the Mamur Zapt's instructions could be stretched. He met Minya every morning now at the
exit from the souk which lay nearest to the Scentmakers' Bazaar,
and they walked together to the school gates. Minya was no longer
accompanied by a senior girl. A senior girl had indeed been chosen
for this task and for several days had walked dutifully beside her.
But then the senior girl had spotted that they were also accompanied by the huge form of this devoted policeman. It was a bit
embarrassing and when Minya one day had suggested that it was
no longer necessary the relieved senior girl had dropped off to
follow her own pursuits, which included a boy in the boys' school.
Minya had felt guilty about this but really, there was no need for
the girl when Selim was so reliable. Like Selim she felt unsure
about whether Selim's remit really ought to include accompanying
her to school every morning. She accused herself of taking the
Mamur Zapt's name in vain and of also corrupting the police force.
She wasn't quite sure what corrupting was, but she felt comfortable having the big policeman beside her. Moreover, he sometimes
gave her sherbet and she liked to suck her finger and put it into
the sherbet powder and then suck it again. She worried that in
some obscure way this might be held to be corruption, too, but
the sherbet was nice and she was sure that there was nothing deeply
wrong with it. She tried to finish the sherbet before she got to the
school gates so no one else knew.

When she saw the Mamur Zapt that morning though, she felt
shaken. The Mamur Zapt, Layla had told her, knew everything
about everything, so he would almost certainly know about the
sherbet, and also the corruption.

Selim, too, was rather shaken when the figure of the Mamur
Zapt suddenly appeared beside him at the school gates. He felt
that some explanation was necessary.

'It was on my way,' he said, 'and I thought I would speak to the little girl and see that she was still all right.'

'And was she?'

'Oh, yes,' Selim assured him.

'Not still worried as much as she was?'

'Oh, no, no! She's fine now.'

'Good. Well, just keep an eye on her as you go past on your patrols. There's no longer a need to make a thing of it, but it's as well to keep an eye open, just in case.'

Selim swore he would keep an eye open and continued on his way, in bliss.

Owen's way was taking him to the Khedivial. To which he had been summoned by the Headmistress. He wondered why, and hoped it was not because there had been another incident like the one that had led to Marie's disappearance. Pausing for a moment outside the door to the Headmistress's study, he felt that old uneasiness from his own school days.

The Headmistress rose to greet him, and, indeed, she should in Egypt, where the men are always a superior figure to the women. In the case of the Headmistress, however, he was not disposed to insist upon it. She was a tall, imposing woman, giving way to no one, and certainly not Mamur Zapt.

She asked how the search for Marie was going. Owen crossed his fingers and said that he hoped they were beginning to get somewhere. The Headmistress nodded. It was having an effect on the school, she said. The initial shock had given way to – she was not quite sure, but she thought that it had been replaced by something deep down which was, in its way, even more worrying. They felt that something ought to have been done by now. It wasn't just impatience, it was as if the shock was still working within them. She had expected the impact to have begun to dwindle, but it hadn't.

Did the girls talk about it, asked Owen.

The Headmistress said that she was sure they did but not as obviously as had been the case at first, They all wanted something to be done; and, with nothing apparent happening, were becoming predisposed to take it upon themselves.

'Like the procession and parade,' said Owen.

'Yes. When they did that, at first I was furious. I wanted to keep them all in or set them a million lines. But then I settled down, and then I began to feel . . . rather proud, actually.'

'Rightly so,' said Owen.

She looked at him.

'You think so? Not everyone does.' She indicated a pile of letters on her desk.

'Letters of protest,' she said. 'Mainly from fathers. "I don't pay to send my daughter to a school where . . ." That sort of thing. I told the girls about them. That was probably a mistake. They all wanted to go home and tell their parents off. The fathers will have found that particularly hard to take. Well, never mind, we'll weather that. However, there is something else I want to discuss with you. Layla has not told me about your allowing her to participate in identifying Marie, but someone else has.'

'I'm sorry. They should not have . . .'

'Told me about it? I'm not bothered about that. What I am bothered about is your using Layla to do something like that. It was not something for a young girl to undertake.'

'I should have used someone else.'

'Yes, you should have.'

'But . . .'

He stopped.

'I can imagine how it went,' she said. 'Layla is a very determined girl. But you shouldn't have allowed it.'

'There was protection, of course.'

'Of course. But still you should not have asked her to do it. She is just a girl. Or was just a girl.'

'What do you mean?'

'She has grown up. Suddenly and too fast. She is no longer a girl now. She is a young woman.'

Next, since he was in that area, he went to the boys' school that Mahmoud had told him about, which young Shawquat had attended, and outside which Marie had sometimes waited for him. He wondered how she had got on. This was a rough area and girls, especially well-to-do girls like Marie, did not go there by themselves.

'The Mamur Zapt?'

The Headmaster looked surprised and more than a little

apprehensive. It was, as Mahmoud had told him, a poor school in a poor area, as so many of them were. Egypt was undergoing a massive educational change from small, religious schools, with Heads whose only claim to knowledge was a thorough acquaintance with the Koran, to a modern system where instruction was given in basic subjects such as mathematics, geography and recent history. The subject matter was new to the teachers and they had had to be specially trained. Their own academic background was usually very limited, so the standard was not very high, although it could be seen to be improving. Teachers' pay was low and they were not well-regarded. And yet they were often dedicated, committed people who believed that the future of Egypt lay in their hands. Mahmoud, who knew them far better than Owen did, admired them; they were kindred to himself, for they believed strongly that they were helping to put the country right.

Although many were devout Muslims, an increasing number were not; this added to the strain between the traditional religious educators and the new, modern, more Western style of education.

The shabbiness of the state system was reflected in the building. The Headmaster shared his study with his other teachers, and, when Owen went in, with two older boys, who were doing more advanced work. It was small, pokey and squeezed for space. Books were piled on the floor, or leaned in drunken columns against the walls. Open exercise books were spread all over the Headmaster's desk. Until recently there had been no exercise books at all. Pupils had written on slates.

'Is it about young Shawquat?' the Headmaster said. 'I hope he has done nothing foolish. He is a good boy. He has just got mixed up with some rather bad ones; not from this school, I hasten to add. And it is not the school's fault, it is the area's. There are too few positive things for them to do, too few good people for them to learn from. There is nowhere for them to go outside school. I sound defensive, I know, and I suppose I am defensive, but in the Geziret there is so much that you have to defend children against. Not least, poverty. I go on too much, I am sorry!'

'At least there is one person who speaks for them,' said Owen, 'and while that is so, they are not without hope.'

'Thank you. You are generous. Too generous. I have overstated things. I tend to do that.'

'It is right that you should. In a place like the Geziret.'

'I wouldn't want to give you the impression that the Geziret is all bad.'

'I know the Geziret.'

The Headmaster sighed.

'In England it must be very different.'

'There are plenty of Headmasters who speak as you do.'

'Headmasters tend to,' he said wryly. 'But, forgive me, we have strayed from what you came to talk to me about. Young Shawquat—'

'Actually, I came to talk to you about music.'

'About music?'

'But also, perhaps, about young Shawquat. He used to play his *nay*, I gather, after school in the playground. Where people came to listen.'

'They did, yes.'

'His schoolfellows. And not just his schoolfellows, children from all around.'

'That is true, yes.'

'And not just children.'

'No. People came out of their houses to listen.'

'Can you tell me about the people?'

The Headmaster looked surprised.

'Well, they were just ordinary people.'

'The Kauris, for instance.'

'We have a lot of Kauris about here. It is a large family.'

'And some of them are good, some bad?'

'As in all families.'

'But some were very bad, lawless in fact?'

'I have to confess that that is true.'

'But still they liked music? Young Shawquat's *nay* playing, for instance?'

'They did, that is so. But why are you asking this?'

'Among the people who came to listen was the Kewfik daughter.'

'She was Ali's friend, yes. She was often here. After school, that is; she went to school first.'

'Yes, a dutiful girl, I think. She would have gone to school first. But there were men who saw her. And saw that she was with young Shawquat. Saw that they were together. Which made it easy.'

'Easy?'

'To seize her one day when she walked home from school.'

The Headmaster was silent. For quite a long time.

'It is possible. But – but – what makes you suppose this?'

'Because young Shawquat told me.'

The Headmaster didn't say anything for some while. Then: 'If he told you that,' said the Headmaster, 'then it is true.'

'They saw her with young Shawquat, and they recognised the girl he was with. They knew that she was a Kewfik and that she was rich. And that her family was. And that they would pay highly for her. So one day, as she was walking home with young Shawquat, after listening to his playing, they seized her.'

'But why did he not say?'

'He was too frightened. So he says.'

'So he says?'

'So he says. One boy against many men. In the Geziret. He knew what happened to people who went against the gang. And I think they threatened him, and told him what would happen, probably to the girl as well as him, if he spoke out.'

'Poor boy!' said the Headmaster.

'And poor girl!' said Owen. 'Now he reproaches himself for not standing up to them. But how could he stand up to them, when they were many and he was one, and he but a boy, a child still in many ways? Nevertheless, he feels that he should have done something. At least spoken to someone. He cannot forgive himself that he did nothing to save the girl, whom he loves, he says, beyond all reason. He tried to run away. He stopped going near her school. He tried to hide, going only to listen to an awalim he favoured. Then creeping away.'

'I can believe it,' said the Headmaster, much agitated. 'In the Geziret you don't talk about what you may have seen, you hold together, presenting a wall to the outside world. It is to them the law, their law, not ours, and adhered to more strongly than ours. He would have feared death, but, more than that, it would be going against the whole Geziret. Even his father would not have

done that! And, besides' – he grimaced – 'have you met his
father? He is not a man who would feel for the girl on this, nor
for his son. He was always against the rich. He would have seen
it as a blow against the mighty. Ali would have had no one to
turn to. Not even his own family.'

'There are other bonds beside family.'

'As strong as family?'

'Music.'

'I do not think even that—'

'In Ali's case.'

'Well, yes, perhaps. But—'

'All the stronger, perhaps, because his family is as it is.'

'It is true that there were several of them who used to hang
around together.'

'And played together, perhaps? Made up a small band? As the
young sometimes do?'

'I can think of—'

'Could you introduce me to them?'

'He was all right. A good player. Should have stayed with us.'

'Are you still a band?'

'It wasn't the same after he left.'

'The *nay* held the band together.'

'First Mustapha drifted away.'

'Then Ahmed.'

'He was no loss. But Mustapha was. With the *nay* gone, and
then the *'ood* . . .'

'We sort of drifted apart.'

'It was that girl.'

'That's what happens,' said Owen sympathetically.

'She was ambitious, that's what was the trouble.'

'Wasn't he?'

'No, not in the way that she was.'

'Have you tried to get him back?'

'He's gone off on his own.'

'Not made a go of it, though.'

'So there's still a chance, then, of you getting back together,'
suggested Owen.

'No, no, it's not like that.'

'Get the girl back,' said Owen. 'That's my advice. Then he'd follow soon enough.'

'No chance!'

'It's not like that.'

'It's always like that,' said Owen. 'People come and go. Especially girls.'

'Yes, that's true,' said someone ruefully.

'You've just got to go on trying,' said Owen.

'No, no, it's not like that. She's locked up.'

'What, some old man has got his eyes on her? And the parents won't let her go out in case she runs off?'

'No, no. She's been snatched.'

'Snatched?'

'Kidnapped.'

'Really?' said Owen sceptically.

'Yes, really.'

'That sort of thing doesn't happen!'

'It does. In the Geziret.'

'Well, I'm – she's not really been kidnapped?'

'She has.'

'Do you know where she's being held? I mean, you could let her out and then you'll be able to get her back. She'd be grateful, and—'

'No, no, it's nothing like that! She's being held by some hard men, who expect to make a lot of money out of her. Really hard men! So you don't want to blunder in there!'

'But you know where she is?'

'Thinking of trying to get her out?'

'Well . . .'

'Don't think it, friend. That way you'll stay alive.'

'I told my girl friend about it, and she said just the same as you. Get her out! And get the money for yourself.'

'Well, I didn't say that actually,' said Owen. 'But it's not a bad idea!'

'Well, she didn't say that exactly. She said they were nasty bastards and it ought not to be allowed. There's a real girl at the end of this and someone ought to get her out. I said to her just what I said to you. "That's the way to get your throat cut," I said. "Men are all the same," she said, "when it comes to dodging responsibility." "Hey, wait a minute," I said. "I'm not like that!" "He'd get her out and then take her home for himself," said one of my mates." "And that's just what I'm afraid of," she said.'

Selim, meanwhile, had been hanging around unobtrusively, just out of earshot but not out of eyeshot. It had become very hot and the sweat was trickling down his face. He sat down in the shade.

No sooner had he sat down than, the next moment, Owen was there! Selim couldn't believe it. The moment you'd taken your weight off your feet he was right next to you.

'Selim,' he said, 'see that man? I want you to follow him. Don't let him see you, but watch where he goes. If it's his own place, so much the better. And then come back and tell me. And if there's a woman there, keep your eye on her especially.'

There was a woman there, who came out into the street and lingered there and then went back into the house with the man. She was a pretty girl – in the Geziret they didn't go in much for veils and he noticed the fact almost automatically – and Selim had no difficulty in keeping his eye on her.

The sun went down and the shadows began to lengthen. The house was a single storey and made of mud brick. There were no windows and the door, as elsewhere in the Geziret, was left open to give not just air but light. Selim wondered whether to go back and report to Owen but decided to stay a little while in case there were any developments.

The only development was that the woman came out with a large jar on her head and an infant on her hip. She went along the street to where a tap was set in the wall and began to fill her pot. When the pot was full she put it back on to her head and went back along the street and into her house.

There were no further developments and it grew dark. Through the door he could see a small flame. From inside the house came a strong smell of garlic and onions. Selim guessed that they were settling down to supper and began to think about his own.

Now it was quite dark. The man came out and went along the street to a restaurant, where people were sitting outside in the street playing dominoes. The man sat down at one of the tables and summoned a pipe.

Selim judged it was time to go back to the Bab-el-Khalk and report to Owen.

Owen knocked on the open door.

'Is anyone within?' he asked.

'The master of the house is out,' said the woman.

She came out into the doorway, then stopped in surprise at the sight of Owen.

'The master is out,' she repeated.

'I know,' said Owen. 'It is you I seek. Do not be alarmed,' he added quickly. 'I come as a friend seeking help for another.'

'Who are you?' she asked, seeing now that he was an Englishman.

'A friend,' he repeated, 'seeking help for another. A woman,' he added significantly.

'Why does she not come herself?'

'She cannot. She is held behind locked doors.'

The woman stepped back.

'This is no business of mine.'

'Ah, but it is! She is a woman in need. Bad men have seized her.'

'If she is a bad woman—'

'She is not. She is a good one. Only very young.'

'Has she no father? No brother?'

'No brother, no. A father, yes. But he is sick, and so I act for him.'

'You are an Englishman. Is she English?'

'No, she is, like yourself, Egyptian.'

'How comes it that you are acting for her?'

'Because no other will do it.'

She hesitated.

'This is a man's business, not mine.'

'It is, if no man will undertake it.'

She half stepped away to go.

'Do not turn from her,' pleaded Owen. 'She is a young girl on her own.'

'Did you say that she is being held?'

'Yes, against her wishes.'

'Why is that? Has some man spoken for her and will she not have him?'

'No one has spoken for her.'

'Not even asked?'

'No. She was seized against her will.'

'That is wrong!'

'It is. And must be stopped. And therefore I have come to you.'

'Why me?'

'Because you have been spoken of as a good woman.'

'If a man has taken her by force . . .'

'Not a man: men.'

'Then that is doubly wrong!'

'It is. And we must stop it!'

'We?'

'Thou and I.'

'I will seek my man's advice!'

'Do not. For he will go with the men who have taken her.'

'My husband is a good man,' she protested vigorously.

'Yes, I think he is: but a frightened one.'

'If he is frightened, why should not I be?'

'I think you will not be. Because you are, like her, a woman. And feel for her as a woman.'

'I do not know her.'

'You probably do. She is the Kewfik girl.'

The woman recoiled.

'Then it is dangerous to have anything to do with her!'

'Even a Kewfik woman is a woman!'

'Why do you act for her?'

'Because she is on her own. And a woman.'

'It is easy for you to talk thus.'

'I know. Easier for me than it is for you.'

'Easier to act, too!'

'I know. But I cannot act without your help.'

'Some other woman—'

'She is in love. With a *nay* player.'

'A *nay* player?'

'Yes. A man of music. As you were, and are, in love with a man of music. So I thought you would understand her.'

'I do. But I cannot do this.'

'All I ask for is information.'

'What information?'

'I need to know where she is.'

'I do not know where she is.'

'I think your husband does, or, at least, he has a pretty good idea of where she might be.'

'He does not tell me such things.'

'I think you could find out.'

'It would cost me – it would cost me my life, and perhaps his!'

'Who would know? My tongue will not tell.'

'You say that . . .'

'I am a man used to holding his tongue. I will not tell. No one will ever know. Not even your husband, unless you tell him.'

'You are asking too much!'

'I ask a great, great deal, I know. But I do not ask for myself. I ask for a young girl on her own without anyone to aid her if you will not.'

'I would like to help her, but . . .'

'I know I ask a great deal. But without help I can do nothing. And I fear that time is running out.'

'Running out?'

'How long will they wish to keep her?'

'Cannot someone pay? Someone can always pay.'

'If someone pays, the men will not release her. They will ask for more.'

'Let them give more, then!'

'And more. Until there is no more left to give. And then, I ask again, how long will they want to keep her?'

'Perhaps they will let her go.'

'If they let her go, do they not increase the danger for themselves? They will fear that she will reveal who they are.'

'I cannot do this. It is too much to ask. My husband – my child – do you know what it is to have a child?'

'Yes, I know what I ask.'

'I cannot do it!'

'Not even for a girl who loves a man of music?'

'Do not ask me more! I – I will think about it.'

* * *

As he was walking back to the Bab-el-Khalk he saw a figure on a donkey coming towards him. It was a woman, and seemed familiar. When she came up to him she saw him looking at her and laughed. Then she pulled back her veil.

It was the Old Woman of the souk.

'Greetings, mother! What are you doing in these unfamiliar parts?'

'Making peace. What are you doing?'

'I make peace too.'

'It is hard work, making peace!'

'It is, indeed!'

'But if the man cannot make it, the task must pass to the women.'

'May God prosper your efforts, mother!'

'And yours, too, Mamur Zapt.'

As she rode on past, a small voice beside him said: 'So you know her, too?'

It was Minya, on her way home from school. Not far away was the burly figure of Selim.

'Why, do you know her?'

'Yes. Quite well. Marie often used to take me in to see her on our way home.'

'Into the souk?'

'Yes. We always used to go through the souk. In the morning, going in, Marie liked to try the perfumes at the Scentmaker. Then in the afternoon, going home, she liked to drop in on the Old Woman and they used to have a chat.'

'And what did they talk about?'

'Life,' said Minya largely. 'Marie was always asking her questions, like "what sort of man should I marry?"'

'And what did the Old Woman say?'

'"Rich",' she said. 'But I don't think she really meant it, because she used to laugh when she said it. And Marie used to say: "That's no use, I'm rich already." And the Old Woman used to say: "Why, then, you'll have to learn how to use it!" And then they both used to laugh. And sometimes the Old Woman would ask me how I would use it. I would buy lots and lots of sherbet, I said. "And then you'd fizz and pop!" Marie used to say.'

'What else did you talk about?'

'What we would be when we grew up – Marie used to talk about that all the time. If she was rich, said the Old Woman, perhaps she should take a lowly job. Then she would learn wisdom, to go with her riches. "Couldn't I do that without having a lowly job?" asked Marie. "Probably not," said the Old Woman. That was the kind of thing they talked about for hours. It got a bit dull after a time, and the Old Woman used to say, "The beginning of wisdom is not to go on too long about it. You'd better take this little one home now, or else she'll fall asleep." "I won't," I used to say, because I'm very good at staying awake! But sometimes I felt quite like it, and I would hear Marie say: "She has." And then there was another woman, who was sometimes there, the awalim, and she would pick me up and sit me on her lap. But in the end we would go home.'

TEN

Georgiades had been hanging around the Kewfik stables for so long that he seemed a part of the furniture. Or perhaps an implement; someone suggested a shovel for piling the dung. At any rate, on whatever terms, they accepted him and no one questioned when he came in, in the morning. He seemed to spend the day sitting in the stables, chatting to everybody. They all accepted him, except perhaps the elder Shawquat, who, like him, talked to everybody, but in a sharper way.

One of the people Georgiades talked to was the widow of the man recently killed. She was getting over her loss – she had never cared greatly for her husband – but said that she had difficulty sleeping at night. Georgiades said that he knew a man in the souk who could give her something for that, and promised to look him up, and that afternoon he went to see his friend in the Scentmakers' Bazaar.

'Certainly!' said the scentmaker. 'I'll make you up something. Strong or weak?'

'Well, I don't know.'

'Strong, if you want her to be asleep and not to know; weak if you just want to soothe her.'

'A bit in-between, I think,' said Georgiades, 'to start with.'

'That's what they all say: to start with.'

'They surely don't want it to be too strong.'

'No, no, and they don't want it to be little. In case she wakes up.'

'But wouldn't he perhaps want her to be a bit awake?'

'There are all sorts of tastes and it depends on whether she's your wife or not.'

'Why does it depend?'

'Well, if she's not your wife, you might prefer her not to know.'

'I think I'll go half way, if you don't mind. In fact, it's not for my wife.'

'Lucky man!'

'No, no, it's not like that. Her husband, you see, was stabbed last week.'

'Oh, I'm sorry.'

'She's not too bothered. She just can't sleep.'

'Stabbed, did you say?'

'Yes. He worked at the Kewfik stables.'

'Oh, I know the man. Some trouble with the Kauri boys.'

'That's right.'

'There's always trouble between the Kewfik and the Kauris. Although they do say there's talk of a truce.'

'Yes, I heard that. It would be a good thing.'

'Oh, I don't know. Bad for business.'

'Bad for— Oh, I see! They come to you to be patched up, do they?'

'It's cheaper than going to the hakim.'

The Greek chuckled.

'You are a one,' he said. 'Seeing it like that!'

'It's the most sensible way to see it. But don't side with either, and then you'll get the business of both.'

'You deserve to make a fortune!'

'Well, I do. But it's not happened yet.'

'Not only that: they throw stones at you!'

'Bastards!'

'Heard anything more about that?'

'No, and not expecting to. Things have gone quiet since they've had this truce.'

'Profits have dropped, have they?'

'They have. Of course, there's always other things. Like love philtres.'

'Or sleeping draughts,' said the Greek, greatly daring.

'Same thing.'

'Really?'

'From my point of view. Same materials. Just a different bottle.'

'You are a one!'

'One way or another, I reckon the Kewfiks and the Kauris keep you in business.'

'Long may it be before they find out!'

Georgiades picked up the package from the counter.

'I'm going over there now. I'll take it for her.'

'Who's paying?'

'Oh, I'll pay. It's not much.'

'I hope you get something in return for your labours!' said the shopkeeper winking.

'The idea of it!' said Georgiades, laughing too.

'Oh, by the way,' said the scentmaker, as he was going out, 'are you going near the stables?'

'Right next door. That's where she lives, and so far they've not put her out.'

'Can you drop something in for me at the stables?'

'A pleasure.'

The scentmaker bent down behind the counter and came up with a package.

'It's for Shawquat.'

'Shawquat? The boy?'

'No. It's the old man. He has lumbago badly. You'd be doing him a favour if you could get this to him.'

'Gladly.'

When they opened the package at the Bab-el-Khalk it was not a surprise.

Georgiades smelt it, then licked his fingers and tasted it.

'Fine quality,' he said appreciatively.

Owen did the same.

'Very fine,' he said. 'I'm surprised there's anyone around here who could afford it.'

'The Kewfiks?'

'I shouldn't think so. The father is a strict Muslim and very strait-laced.'

'Marie?'

'I doubt it. She kicks over the traces and seems willing to have a go at most things. But among all the Khedivial girls, I think it would have come out. She may have sampled it at some point, but this isn't a sample. It's a whacking great load, fit for a palace.'

'Where the Kewfiks live is a palace.'

'The package was addressed to Shawquat.'

'He won't have wanted it for himself. He'll be feeding it on to others, spreading it around.'

'Could we check? You ask around in the stables.'

'I haven't seen any signs of it.'

'And it's very fine quality. Not the sort of stuff you'd be taking if you were a hand at the stables.'

'The Court? Fed out through the mother?'

'Unlikely. But possible. She would have the contacts but my impression is that she doesn't go in for that sort of thing.'

'Money?'

'Well, the Kewfiks are not badly off.'

'They may be now. With that nephew running the family finances.'

'He won't really be running them. The bank will be doing it or keeping a tight hold. Besides, his father is a *very* strict Muslim and also a disciplinarian. He'll be watching Ali Osman like a hawk. He lets him spread money around but dribbles it out to him.'

'All the more reason for him wanting to deal.'

'Somehow I don't see it. He'd be terrified of his father. Still, you could check.'

'We keep coming back to Shawquat.'

'Who is also a very strict Muslim.'

'Strict enough to worry about who he feeds it out to?'

'It's a big quantity. This would not be little users.'

'A big user, then?'

'Or a big purpose.'

Nikos reported that things had suddenly gone quiet. The kidnappers had made no attempt to contact him. Nor had the bank been approached. Nor had Ali Osman.

'If only I had been,' Ali Osman said. 'All this talk of money and I can't get my hands on any of it. Besides, in a strange way I'm worried about this girl. Does it mean that—? Surely not! They wouldn't have killed her, not at this stage in the negotiations. And while they're talking, there's hope. Goodness me, that's nearly a witticism isn't it? Most unusual for me! Actually I think it's something that you were saying. Keep talking, that's what you said, while you're doing whatever you are doing, which, judging by results so far, doesn't seem to be much.'

Although he didn't say it, Owen was worried too about the

silence. There was always the risk in this kind of negotiation that the talks would collapse, that the kidnappers would panic and walk away. And if they did walk away, it probably wouldn't be with clean hands.

And then, suddenly, contact was resumed and the talks started again.

This was not uncommon in negotiations like these. The kidnappers' side would waver, there would be arguments about how to proceed, some would want to drop out, some to press on.

Nikos decided to refresh their minds about the possible rewards of a successful outcome and signalled that he might be prepared to release the cash now. Of course, he wouldn't. He would just release some of it. He offered a sum as guarantee of good faith. Naturally, they said it was too small, and wanted more. Nikos refused. There was a bit of blustering and threatening, but Nikos was adamant. Not unless, he threw in as an afterthought, he could be sure that Marie was still all right. And for that he would need to see her.

A short silence followed, and then further blustering. And then they agreed. On the same basis as before, with the same personnel. Selim's wife was called upon once again. Looking at her broad shoulders and hefty arms, Owen almost thought he could dispense with the men standing by.

Selim, surprisingly, was showing signs of being the weak link. It was one thing going into the breach himself, it was another letting his wife do that. Fatima, who was now quite enjoying herself, overruled him and Selim went into a sulk, from which he was rescued only by running into Minya, who wanted to dance with him. Fatima, who was there waiting for her further instructions, wanted to dance too, and for several minutes the Bab-el-Khalk was regaled by the sight of one man-mountain and one woman-mountain, skipping in the forecourt. This did have the effect of settling everybody's nerves and things could once more go ahead.

No doubt similar things were happening on the kidnapper's side.

The parties met and Marie was produced. The only hitch was that, following the intervention of the Khedivial Headmistress, Layla was at first not to be in attendance. However, the kidnappers insisted on sticking by the original terms. Consent was sought from both Layla and the Headmistress and refused by the Headmistress until Layla went and had some bracing words with her, after which the Headmistress backed down.

Minya, who had hung around after the dancing, hoping for more, wanted to participate too, but this was ruled out by all sides.

So, in the end, all went ahead as planned. Marie, wan and thinner and very pleased to see Layla but otherwise unchanged, seemed to be holding up. Layla, rebellious beneath a burka, was grimly determined and disposed to tell the kidnappers how they should be doing things. It was, as the kidnappers pointed out, now only a question of cash.

Certainly, Nikos agreed: but in what form?

The kidnappers were taken aback. In their hands, that was what they wanted. It was a lot of money and there could be difficulties in raising it at short notice. It was definitely there, the bank assured everybody, but if small notes were required, amassing enough of them would take time. And if, as the kidnappers seemed to be suggesting, payment was to be in coin, that would take time too. (Nikos had been instructed to play for time, which any bureaucrat in Egypt was only too glad to do.) Nikos pointed out that the portage of so many milliemes on the backs of donkeys and camels would also take time.

Layla, whose nerves, and certainly temper, were wearing thin, flew off the handle and denounced the banks, Nikos and the government for mucking about; the kidnappers expressed their astonishment at finding such perceptiveness and intelligence in a woman. Two of them immediately proposed to her. Layla, growing wilder by the second, bought time by agreeing that there were things to be said for such an idea, but pointed out that because of her age and the new iniquitous requirements of the hated British, forms would have to be filled in and this, too, would take time. And she was not at all convinced the Headmistress would be prepared to agree.

The kidnappers sensed that they were getting to the heart of power. It was clear that Layla had her finger on the pulse of the great, and must, indeed, be a player of stature herself: a conclusion reinforced by seeing that Nikos was so frightened of her.

The two kidnappers who had previously offered marriage to her, now carried away by their visions, upped their offer by promising improbable numbers of camels in addition.

Their leader, whose head was now beginning to swirl with possibilities, began to consider whether, if this girl was so powerful, they might not do better to kidnap her rather than Marie.

Positions began to wobble.

Owen, sensing they were now on the brink of something, sent in coffee all round and left them all to sweat.

The two men who had proposed to Layla were the first to crack. The enormity of what they were proposing struck home and they withdrew their offers.

Their leader sent a message, scrawled by finger on the coffee grounds of the bottom of a saucer, outlining his new proposals. Only to receive a sharp rebuff from above hidden beneath a slice of Turkish delight, and an injunction to stop messing about and get on with it.

Nikos declared that they were almost there and that untold riches were ready to pour upon them. Because of their demand for payment in small coins, however, it was taking the bank longer than it had anticipated to amass the money. It was having to send to Sennar to find the necessary milliemes. They were on their way, however, and provided there were no more eccentric provisos imposed by the kidnappers at this late moment, the money would be ready in three days.

Three days? The kidnappers were aghast. Nikos, however, (having checked with Owen that three days would be enough) was adamant. Did they think that milliemes in this quantity were like grains of sand in the desert, that it was simply a matter of scooping them up?

Three days it was; and before they could change their mind Nikos adjoined the meeting.

Marie, tearful at the last, and clinging on to Layla, was persuaded to leave, with Layla, spitting fire, led in the opposite direction.

Nikos heaved a sigh of relief, although it was uncertain whether this was a natural reaction to a long, hot, arduous day or just relief at getting away from Layla.

At the meeting afterwards in the Bab-el-Khalk he offered the view that the kidnappers were coming to the end of their tether, although possibly this was more a reflection of his feeling than theirs.

Owen began to worry whether the three-day time limit to have imposed on himself would be enough, and started contingency planning in case it were not.

Ali Shawquat had meanwhile been giving music lessons to the el Zaki children, with Aisha in anxious attendance, although at a sensible distance. The boy was taking his teaching very seriously and the children liked his lessons and were making good progress.

Then, one afternoon, Ali Shawquat announced that he was taking the afternoon off. The children would be resting, as they always did in the afternoon, so their studies would not be affected.

Aisha was quite happy for him to take the afternoon off. After all, the rest of Egypt was. Young Ali, however, showing unexpected signs of his father's strict work ethic, felt uneasy about it. He was not just taking the afternoon off, he explained: he had an important purpose in mind. Under Aisha's gentle persuasion he confessed that he was going to 'do something' about Marie. He had allowed her to be taken, he said, and that was not a manly thing to do. (More echoes of his father.) He had failed her once but now he was going to put that right.

Aisha praised his resolve but urged the necessities for caution. If his efforts were going to bring him up against evil men he should proceed with care. She did not want him, and nor, she was sure, would Marie, to get hurt. And she felt that, given the nature of these wicked men, that was all too likely. Ali Shawquat, moved, kissed her hand and said that he would take every precaution but that this was something he had to do. Would he not take counsel from her husband first? Ali paused. He would have liked to have done whatever he was going to do independent of the advice of others. The trouble was that he couldn't quite think what he was going to do. Something brave and worthy anyway.

This idea of consulting her husband was, perhaps, not such a bad idea. Ali was used to forbidding fathers, and so he wasn't that sure about Mahmoud. He had always been courteous and pleasant to Ali – but he was pleasant and courteous to everybody.

Even his wife. Ali, by this time, would have died for Aisha. But he couldn't quite understand why Mahmoud wasn't firmer with her. After much thought he had come to the conclusion that his was, perhaps, the modern way. He had noticed that Owen seemed to address his wife, Zeinab, in similar terms. Could this be the modern thing to do? Ali hoped it was. There was too much shouting and too many blows in the Geziret. He wouldn't, he decided, treat Marie like that.

He was disconcerted, when finally he plucked up enough courage to call in on Mahmoud at his office, to find him closeted with Owen. This was off-putting. Owen was not just police, he was English. For a moment Ali wondered if Mahmoud was a traitor. Then he recalled being told that he was an ardent Nationalist. How did that square with the two of them being friends? The English were the enemy, surely? His father had told him that repeatedly. *Everyone* said that! Yet here Owen and Mahmoud were, apparently on the friendliest of terms. Not only that but Owen was married to Aisha's friend Zeinab, clearly an Egyptian. How could that be?

Now that he came to think of it, Aisha had not actually said that Owen and Zeinab were married. It was rather that they were close friends. Even lovers? This was bad, and typically English. Zeinab must be one of the women that his father continually fulminated about, immoral, immodest, etc. Ali would bet that she didn't wear a burka! And then he recollected that he had caught a glimpse of her once, leaving Aisha's house. She certainly had not been wearing a burka then. But, the troubling memory came to him, she *had* been wearing a veil. Granted it was one of those slight, filmy ones the sophisticated Cairo ladies wore, the sort that made your knees knock, but it was a veil nonetheless.

Ali felt that he was floundering in deep waters.

'But I thought you were enemies,' he said.

'We are, we are!' said Owen. 'But also friends.'

'We work together,' said Mahmoud.

'Often,' said Owen. 'But not always.'

'What happens when you don't?'

'The country seizes up,' said Owen. 'So we have to.'

Ali shook his head in bewilderment.

'But are you not British?'

'I work for the Khedive.'

'How can you?'

'If you played in an orchestra,' said Owen, 'and someone came from another country and asked you to play for them, wouldn't you do so?'

'It is not the same thing,' said Mahmoud.

Owen laughed.

'No, it is not,' he agreed. 'Nevertheless, we both play in the same orchestra.'

'The orchestra comes by invitation.'

'So do the British,' said Owen. 'In theory.'

'It is a fiction,' said Mahmoud.

'We argue about this between ourselves all the time,' said Owen.

'But never get anywhere,' said Mahmoud. 'The British are still here.'

'My father says the Khedive is a traitor,' said Ali Shawquat.

'And many would agree with him,' said Mahmoud.

'But some would not,' said Owen.

Ali shook his head in bemusement.

'I think I will stick to music,' he said.

'What was it you came to see me about,' asked Mahmoud.

'Marie,' said Ali.

'There we are all playing in the same orchestra,' said Mahmoud.

Owen said that he would withdraw if it made it easier for Ali to say what he wanted to say.

'It might be better,' said Mahmoud. 'But don't go too far. I want to talk to you.'

Owen went out.

'Well?' said Mahmoud.

It was hard for Ali to put it into words.

'I want to do something,' he said, 'for Marie. It is my fault that she was taken. I should have stopped them.'

'How could you?' asked Mahmoud.

'I don't know. And I still don't know. I thought I would go to them and plead with them.'

'What can you offer them?'

'Nothing,' said Ali. 'I have only music. But one or two of

them praised my playing. And I thought, if I went to them, perhaps they would let her go. For the sake of the music.'

Mahmoud shook his head.

'I don't think so,' he said.

'I don't think so, either,' agreed Ali sadly. 'But it is all I can offer. I have no money. And I know that is what they really want. I thought . . .'

He fell quiet for a moment, then went on.

'I thought if I went to them and offered myself, that would, perhaps, satisfy them.'

'It won't,' said Mahmoud.

'I know that too, deep down,' said Ali, 'but what do I do?'

'You know who they are and where they are,' said Mahmoud. 'You could tell me.'

'And what would you do? Tell the Mamur Zapt?'

'If you don't want me to, I won't.'

'He would put them in prison,' said Ali.

'And would free Marie,' said Mahmoud.

'They are my friends,' whispered Ali. 'They were my friends. I cannot betray them.'

'Are you not betraying Marie if you don't?'

'What shall I do?' said Ali desperately. 'What can I do? What ought I to do?'

'That is what you must decide.'

'If I went to my father, he would say: "They are ordinary men from the Geziret. You must go with them. Not with a daughter of the Kewfiks."'

'And what do you think?'

'I think I will go to them and say: "Release her or I shall tell."'

'And what will they do?'

'They will kill me.'

'How would that help Marie?'

'I don't know, but – but it is the right thing to do.'

'I don't think it is the right thing to do.'

'You do not live in the Geziret.'

Mrs Shawquat had not seen her son for some time and was worried.

'You have frightened him away with your roughness,' she said to her husband.

'The boy would take fright at his own shadow,' Shawquat replied. 'He is no boy of mine.'

'I wish you had told me before that you would not own him,' his wife replied with spirit. 'Then I could have found someone else!'

'Perhaps you did find someone else,' Shawquat said. 'And that is why I have a boy like him.'

'He takes after me. He has brains.'

Shawquat snorted.

'He is a waster,' he said. 'He will never come to anything.'

'His talents are different from yours.'

'Talents! Is that what they are? He keeps them well-hidden!'

'He has not been here for over a month. And he has been going around with bad men who will do him harm. You must speak to him.'

'What good would that do? He goes his own way and will not listen to me.'

'That is because you speak to him so roughly.'

'I speak to him as I am. And he has been my son long enough to know how I am.'

'You must try again. Or he will slip from us.'

'He has already slipped. Nevertheless, I will speak to him.'

If he could find him, Shawquat thought. He had not spoken to him for weeks. He had a moment of misgiving, that was not right. It was not as it should be. The boy should come home at night. Not forever listening to or making music. What good would that do in the world? How would it help Egypt? He, himself, Shawquat, devoted his life to doing things for Egypt, while the boy did nothing. He knew that they talked about the boy in the stables, mocking him, no doubt. And if you mocked the son, you mocked the father. People would see the son and say: 'Is that your new Egypt?'

He had wanted a son who would stand by him, and help him bring change to Egypt. There were, Allah knew, so many things to be done. And perhaps now, more than at any other time, they might be achieved. Shawquat had worked for them all his life, first as a trade union organiser and then on his own.

He had gathered a small group around him and now they were

beginning to get somewhere. Others were beginning to join him, even if his son wasn't. He had the Kewfik boys with him, and would soon have the Kauri boys. And others. He was sure there were many who felt like him. They would stand up at the right moment. And the moment would be soon!

But there was so much to do. How would he find time when his wife was pressing him to spend time talking to his son? Had he not talked enough to his son?

But the boy would not listen. He did not share his father's plans and hopes. He did not care, that was the nub of it. He did not care enough about Egypt. All he cared about was playing the *nay*. His wife should speak to the boy about that. It was not for him to speak to the boy about things he had so often spoken to him about, it was for the boy now to listen.

Things were at last afoot. If the lads would stop fighting and killing each other and concentrate instead on killing the enemy. The British did not fight each other, did they? But the Egyptians did, all the time. How could you make progress when people were forever standing aside or fighting their friends?

People talk of peace, and so they should: peace was right. But only if it was a good peace: a peace that would enable you to build a new Egypt!

Things were beginning to move, he could feel it in his bones. The lads were coming together.

Except . . .

What was this about the Old Woman of the souk? Getting in the way? She and the other women? What did they know about it? Listen to them and you would never get anything done. They sat back on their arses and worried about their sons! They were just getting in the way!

Even his own wife, who had once stood shoulder to shoulder with him throwing stones at the British, who had worked tirelessly with him for a better Egypt, who he had always believed thought exactly as he did – now even she was talking of the Old Woman of the souk, who was riding around on her donkey getting in the way of all the good things he was doing. This was not a matter, he told her, for women. And she told him to his face that quarrelling was for women too, that often only they could put it right. Foolish talk – women's talk!

And now the boy. Instead of binding to his father, as all boys would naturally do, he was moving away from him. And turning to a Kewfik daughter, of all things! What had the Kewfiks ever done for the Shawquats? What had they ever done for Egypt? They had not put in, they had only taken out. They had enriched themselves at the expense of others. The Pashas were all the same, taking from the poor and giving to the rich.

Those kidnappers were on the right lines. Take the money from the Pashas and use it for the Egyptians as a whole! That was what it was all about. They and he were working on similar lines.

But the boy – he kept coming back to the boy. Why could he not see what was to be done? What he ought to be doing? Instead of puffing into his *nay*!

What had he done to deserve a boy like that? A boy who stood aside when Egypt needed him?

ELEVEN

The fan wasn't working this morning in the seniors' room and tempers were growing short.

'Why does it always have to be *English* history?'

'It doesn't. This morning we are doing the Crusades,' said the Headmistress, who happened to be taking the lesson that morning.

'All Richard the Lionheart and that sort of stuff?'

'Not this morning,' said the Headmistress unruffled. 'He's in prison.'

'Best place for him!'

'How long does he have to stay there?'

'Years and years,' said Layla. 'Until his ground-down subjects have got enough money together to pay the ransom for him.'

'Ransom?'

There was an awkward silence. Everyone thought of Marie. Officially there had been no talk of a ransom. Unofficially, in the school, there had been talk of little else.

'At least he got out,' said one of the girls quietly.

'How? By paying the ransom?'

'Yes, but before they could do that,' said Layla, 'they had to find out where he was. All they knew was that he was locked up in a castle somewhere. But he had a faithful minstrel who went round all the castles playing his favourite songs outside. Until one day he heard someone inside joining in. And he knew it was Richard.'

'I'll bet!'

'It's just a story, of course,' said the Headmistress. 'But it's a nice one.'

Over in the corner of the classroom there was a sudden commotion and several of the girls stood up.

'What is it now?'

'A scorpion.'

'A scorpion? Surely not!'

'It's just a baby one. It must have been in one of the deliveries for the stores.'

'Can someone get rid of it? Khabradji, you're nearest.'

'I hate scorpions!'

'It's just a baby. It won't hurt you.'

'Oh yes it will! Our cook got stung last week. She put her hand into some onions she'd just bought in the souk—'

'Well, that was daft, wasn't it?'

'—and there was a scorpion in them, a little one, just a baby, like ours, and she got stung on her finger, and it was so painful that she screamed, you could hear the screams all through the house, and she put her finger in boiling water—'

'What did she do that for?'

'—and didn't feel a thing!'

'Oh, come on, Khabradji!'

'That is what she said! And we could hear the screams all through the house.'

'All right, all right, Khabradji, spare us the dramatics.'

'So, I'm not going to touch it, that's all!'

'No one's asking you to touch it. Slip a sheet of paper under it, open the window and throw it out!'

'The window's stuck!'

'Oh, for goodness' sake! Just give it a shake. Melusine, you do it.'

'It really is stuck!'

'Harder! That's it!'

'It's coming! It's all right now!'

'Throw it out! There it goes! I hope you break your back, you little bastard!'

'Melusine!'

'Shut the window or it will fly back in!'

'They don't fly. They crawl. Watch your feet, everybody!'

More pandemonium.

'All right, all right! That will do. Back to your places every-body! Now, where were we?'

'In the Bloody Tower, I think, with Richard,' said Layla.

'Why is the tower bloody?' asked someone hopefully.

'Sit down, everybody! Sit down!'

*   *   *

'Well, old friend,' said the shopkeeper in the Scentmakers' Bazaar, 'it's good to see you. Come back for more?'

'My wife's afraid she will run out,' said the apparently slow Greek.

'No chance of that, I would have thought. Still, I'll put some extra ones in this time.'

'Thank you. She does seem to be getting through them rather quickly. "They've all got to be paid for," I told her.'

'Ah, but a little order like this won't break the bank,' said the Scentmaker. 'By the way, did you deliver that other package for me?'

'To Mr Shawquat? I did, and he was very grateful.'

'And so am I, my friend!'

'It was nothing,' said the slow Greek modestly, 'Glad to help.'

'I had a man who would deliver for me. But he got killed.'

'Killed?'

'Yes. Stabbed. Poor Hamid!'

'Yes, I think I've heard about him. A man at the Kewfik stables, wasn't it?'

'That's right. Poor Hamid! Stabbed. In the street!'

'Got into a quarrel, did he?'

'Yes, and then got stabbed. For no reason at all! He used to deliver for me. I shall miss him. Of course, that's not the important thing. What matters is the family he leaves behind him.'

'Children, were there?'

'Seven. A lot for a woman to manage on her own.'

'The stables will help, won't they? Didn't you say he worked at the Kewfik stables?'

'He did. And they will look after her for a bit. But only a bit. You can't expect them to do it for ever.'

'The Kewfiks are quite generous in that way, I've heard.'

'Well, they are. But there are limits.'

'What was the quarrel about, I wonder?'

'I don't know. There are always quarrels among the stablemen, and these quarrels affect us all. Me, for instance.'

'It will affect your deliveries.'

'It will. I've got quite a few of them, and it all adds up. Of course, as I said, that's not the main consideration.'

'The family?'

'And Hamid himself. I shall miss him.'

'Of course.'

'You get to know a person when you work with them for a long time. You get to depend on him. And now that he's gone . . .'

'Well, I don't mind dropping the occasional package in for you. Occasional, of course.'

'You're not looking for a job?'

'I'm afraid not. But glad to help out.'

'You're like that, I know. A decent man, and much appreciated.'

Georgiades dropped in on the widow as he went back to the stables.

'So how's it going?'

'Badly.'

'Heard anything from the Kewfiks yet?'

'Not a thing.'

'Well, of course, with the master in hospital . . .'

'He's got a wife, hasn't he? And Abdullah is supposed to be running things in the stable yard while he's away.'

'Isn't he running things?'

'Yes, but only little things. The stables run themselves really, and Abdullah lets them run.'

'He doesn't do anything new?'

'Never did, of course.'

'All the same, a little money for you, now that Hamid's gone, would be only right.'

'You would have thought so. Hamid worked for them for twenty years.'

'No money at all yet?'

'Only what I've put by myself. That won't go far, with all the mouths to feed.'

'Of course, the Kauris are the ones who should be paying. They're the ones who killed him.'

'They will be paying, the Old Woman says. They've agreed to do that. But how much has still to be settled.'

'The Old Woman of the souk, is this?'

'Yes. She's the go-between and the good thing about having her is that once it's agreed, it's agreed. Both sides abide by what she says.'

'No argument after that?'

'That's right. And it's a blessing for such as me, who hasn't anyone to speak up for them.'

'And in the end, the more that have been party to it the better. There's less chance of anyone slipping back.'

'That's just what the Old Woman said to me!'

'She's a wise old bird.'

'She is.'

'She knows what's going on.'

'She does.'

'Tell me, is the scentmaker in on this? Because he ought to be. Ought to be making a bit of a contribution to you too. Because Hamid did quite a lot of work for him. It would be only fair.'

'Well, yes it would. I never thought of that!'

'I wonder if the Old Woman has thought of it? It's a question of fairness, isn't it? It is wrong to leave people out. Especially those who did a lot of the work. And Hamid was one of those.'

'He certainly was. He was always carrying loads for the scentmaker.'

'I know. I carried one myself after Hamid was gone. It's not a thing I'd want to do regularly, but I thought I'd give the scentmaker a hand when Hamid went. Just for the once when he was left in the lurch.'

'Well, he was. He depended on Hamid.'

'It was a big package. Quite heavy, and do you know what? I thought it was for you. Scent, you know. But there seemed rather a lot of it.'

The woman laughed.

'Scent? For me? That would be the day!'

'But then I saw that it was addressed to Shawquat.'

'Yes, they mostly were.'

'Scent? For Shawquat?'

'It wasn't scent.'

'No, I suppose it wasn't. But – if it wasn't scent, what was it?'

'Hashish, I'll bet. Or some other thing.'

'Of course! Even so, I'm surprised. I didn't think Shawquat was the sort of man.'

'Oh, it wasn't for him.'

'Who was it for then?'

'Ali Fingari.'

'Ali Fingari? The old man? Osman Kewfik's uncle?'

'Yes.'

'Well, I'm surprised. I didn't think he was a hashish user. I thought he was a strict man!'

'Oh, he is a strict man. Never takes any himself. He changes it into money – that's where Shawquat comes in – and uses the money to buy political support. Or so Hamid said. He was always meddling in politics.'

She stopped suddenly.

'Yes?'

She laid a finger on her lips.

'Hamid said that in the end the money finished up with the Khedive himself . . . I don't know if that's true or not. There's so much going on in Court circles that you never really know. But that's what Hamid thought. He said they were always playing politics and for politics you need money.'

'There's truth in that.'

'Mind you, it may just have been talk. There's a lot of wild talk about in the souk. There always is. And I don't know that Hamid knew more about it than anyone else. But it's what he said. And he was nearer to the whole business than most people.'

'Too near, do you think? Was that why he was killed?'

She looked at him for a moment in shock. Then she put her finger back over her lips.

'I don't know. It's best not to know these things. He was always a good man to me.'

Owen went over to the area where the Kauri boys lived. As he was entering it he met the Old Woman coming out.

'Why, mother!' he said. 'What brings you here?'

'The same as what bring you here, I suspect.'

'And what is that?'

'Music,' she said. 'Could it be music?'

'Music? No, I don't think so. Ought it to be?'

'That depends on what you are looking for.'

'I was looking for the reason why the Kauri boys killed Hamid.'

'Ah. In that case, music won't help you.'

'Nevertheless, I am interested in what you might have to tell me about music.'

'I am not sure that I have anything to tell you about music.'

'But you think that I should be thinking about music?'

'It is always good to think about music.'

'Even now, when I am thinking about something else?'

'It is a question of what you think is the most important. I had thought that your mind was on something else.'

'One thinks about many things.'

'If one is a thinking person, yes.'

'As you are, mother.'

'I hope so. At the moment I am just talking and listening.'

'To some purpose, I hope.'

'I hope so, too.'

'And are you succeeding?'

'I think so. Little by little. Mamur Zapt, I am surprised that you have not involved yourself in this before.'

'I was leaving it to you.'

She laughed.

'So like a man!'

'Knowing you could do it better.'

'Well, we'll see. What I have been trying to do is not just end the matter of Hamid's killing sensibly – which I think I shall do – but also end this stupid dispute between the Kewfiks and the Kauris in a way that means it doesn't come up again.'

'The children will bless you, mother, if you can achieve that.'

'And do not bother about the price for Hamid. That is seen to.'

'Good. I do not like a woman being left to manage on her own.'

'She won't be. The souk looks after its own.'

'And the man who killed Hamid?'

'It is best not to ask.'

As she rode away on her little donkey Owen thought how tired she looked. Understandably, if she had been spending all morning reasoning with the Kauris. He wondered now if he should go in to the Kauris or whether the Old Woman had done all that was necessary. In the end he decided that it might blur the message if he went in now. He looked up the street for a coffee house that he might go to.

There wasn't one, but he could see, under the palm trees, a native restaurant. It consisted of a large round tray with a dip in the middle for the charcoal and shallow sides across which had been lain pieces of meat for cooking and the vegetables that Egyptians loved: artichokes, beans, onions. From somewhere came a heavy smell of garlic. There were several people squatting on the ground round it. They took in at once that he was an Effendi, nevertheless made space for him courteously. He thanked them and squatted down. All sorts of people sat at these pavement restaurants, rich, poor, old, young. They were convivial places, as good for a chat as for food. One drank water, and that was the big snag of such places. The water was always lukewarm. Some served tea or coffee and they were somewhat better bets.

A ripple of wind ran through the palm leaves above and then stirred the air on the pavement.

The owner of the restaurant came round to take his order. Owen indicated a piece of meat impaled on a spike and the man served it with lettuce. Some were afraid of eating from the common dish like this but Owen had always found the food clean and wholesome.

He fell into conversation with his neighbour. Owen remarked that he had just seen the Old Woman of the souk.

'A good woman!' he said.

'She is.'

'And it does my heart good to see that she is well. This is wisdom on the part of the Kauris.'

'And on the part of the Kewfiks,' said his neighbour. 'For it takes two to end a quarrel.'

Owen concurred.

'Would that all quarrels could be resolved like this!'

'True.'

They were all elderly men and that was probably why they could talk about such things peaceably. Or perhaps it was that he himself was growing older and found he could talk easily with the Egyptian of the streets. He put this to his neighbour, who at once concurred. Several other men joined in.

'As one grows older, one grows into wisdom,' one said.

'Even Effendis!' said Owen. There was a general mutter of support.

'To a man who walks through the streets,' said Owen, 'and who sees so much good, it hurts when one sees evil fall on a man like Hamid.'

He had wondered if they would know of Hamid, but they seemed to, for they nodded in agreement.

'I cannot but wonder how it came about, since from all I hear Hamid was a man of good standing and did not act rashly.'

'It came about,' said a man sitting opposite him, 'not because he acted rashly but because he was with another who did. This man knew he was carrying something he should not have been carrying and demanded roughly to have some of it for himself. And Hamid said: "It is not mine to give." But the man spoke again and snatched it and Hamid was angry. And when Hamid tried to fend him off the man stabbed him.'

'That was bad!'

'It was very bad. For these things do not have borders built around them and one thing affects another. Hamid was a Kewfik man and when he was killed, the Kewfiks might want recompense.'

'It could have spread further,' said Owen. 'As you rightly said, these things do not have borders. It was wise of the elders to call in the Old Woman.'

They all agreed with that.

'An old head holds wisdom!'

'Sitting where she does, she sees much and hears much. And then she thinks on it before speaking.'

'That is wise,' said Owen. 'And I wish I did the same.'

There were mutters of agreement.

'But when she speaks,' Owen went on, 'it is not always clear to me what she is saying.'

Again there were mutters of agreement.

'Take, for instance, the business of the Shawquat boy and the Kewfik girl. You know what I am talking about? The *nay* player and the rich girl? You have heard the story? Well, in case you haven't, I will tell you. There was once – there still is – a poor *nay* player, who fell in love with a rich girl and she in love with him. Wiser heads knew that this would end badly. But these were not wise heads, they were young heads. And some bad men observed them and decided to seize the girl and make off with her. So they took her from the boy.'

'I know the boy,' said someone. 'It is Ali Shawquat.'

'That is the boy. And the girl—'

'The Kewfik daughter.'

'The boy pines for her. As well he might, for she is a beautiful girl, but a rich one, and there is no hope for the boy, as he is but a poor *nay* player.'

'He is a good *nay* player, you have not said that!'

'Let me say it now. For that touches on the very thing I wanted to ask you as men of experience and wisdom, chosen in the Geziret as elders. We have a poor boy and a rich girl, the one a *nay* player and the other a woman from a family of standing: can we bring the two together? Or are they doomed forever to be apart? Can wealth match itself with poverty, a Kewfik with a Kauri, people of one blood with people of another? Questions difficult enough: so I thought I should seek help. And I put them to the Old Woman of the souk, for I thought surely she will know. But when I spoke with her, she answered in riddles. "Listen to the music!" she said. Now I ask you: what did she mean? For I am lost.'

There was a silence.

Then the man who had spoken before said again: 'He is a good *nay* player. I know the boy.'

'But would you let him be your guide?'

'He is just a boy. A good boy, but still just a boy.'

'Would you follow him?'

'He is just a dreamer.'

'Who knows how he may grow up?'

'He has got a long way to go before I would follow him!'

'What about his father? Is his father a good man?'

'You know his father: Shawquat?'

'I wouldn't follow him!'

'No one is asking you to. The question is about the boy.'

'No, it's not. It's about the music. "Listen to the music." That is what the Old Woman said.'

'How will this help you? Music is music, and we are talking of leadership and counsel.'

'I wouldn't go to a boy for either of these!'

'Nor to his father. If that is what we are talking about.'

'But that is not what we are talking about. "Listen to the music," the Old Woman said. Not "listen to the men"!'

'How can you listen to the music and not to the men?'

'Sometimes the music knows more than the men!'

'I think that is nonsense!'

'No, it makes a sort of sense. It sees deeper than men do.'

'You've lost me!'

'And I can see how that could be so. For doesn't the man make the music?'

'Sometimes he makes deeper than he knows.'

'Well . . .'

The discussion continued to go round in circles.

'I think the Old Woman is a bit cracked.'

'But sometimes she speaks sense. Otherwise why did we ask her to help us?'

'She's quite good when she's got her feet on the ground.'

'But how do you know when she's got her feet on the ground?'

'I've always thought the Old Woman was a bit overrated.'

The conversation went on for some time. It remained inconclusive.

Layla was giving the seniors the benefit of her views.

'As a strategy,' she said, 'it wasn't completely daft. They hadn't got much to go on,' she said, 'only that Richard loved music. He probably sang himself.'

'They probably sang together,' suggested someone.

'They probably did,' said Layla. 'Or would have, if there had been someone else around. Only there wasn't. Remember, he's been locked up. In a cold prison cell. Probably for months, if not years. And he would be getting pretty bored. So when someone outside started singing, he might well be tempted to join in.'

'They could sing a duet. Or maybe a trio if there were three of them. Which there could be if one was playing the music. A lute, or something.'

'A harp, perhaps?'

'Or a drum to get his attention.'

'It could have been a drum. Or maybe Blondel – he was the minstrel – did it all on his own. Playing and singing and walking round castle after castle, in the sun and the sand. And then on to the next one.'

'With never a response – it must have been pretty depressing. Because, remember he was doing this for years and years. And getting nowhere.'

'He must have loved Richard very much.'

'He did. There was probably a bond between the two of them, the King and his minstrel!'

'As well as all the bonds of fealty and loyalty – those bonds were very important in the Middle Ages—'

'Yes, I've read that bit, too!'

'—until one day—!'

'How would they hear each other, locked up like that?'

'Open the window. They could always open a window!'

'No, they couldn't! There weren't any windows. Not windows like we have.'

'Just a space in the wall!'

'Well, that would make it easier to hear, wouldn't it?'

'*Anyway*, one of them heard and sang back, Richard, I imagine. And then Blondel sang back. A sort of duet, yes, if you must, Esmeralda.'

'Or a trio, if there were three of them!'

'The point is,' said Layla, 'that it was through Blondel doing this that they found out that Richard was inside—'

'Pining away, with only a rat to keep him company.'

'All right, Esmeralda!'

'It's a lovely story!' she sighed.

'But it's not true!'

'Oh, I don't know. It could be.'

'Think of it,' said Layla, 'as a strategy.'

'But there aren't any castles for us to sing outside. And if there were, Marie wouldn't be inside them!'

'It doesn't have to be a castle. It could be any old place.'

'There would be no point in us singing in any old place!'

'We would have to sing in some place where she was likely to be.'

'But we don't know where she is likely to be!'

'We know it's somewhere in the Geziret.'

'We don't even know that, really.'

'I suppose I could ask the Mamur Zapt,' said Layla, confident in her new contacts. 'He doesn't know precisely, but he's probably got some idea. Which is more than we have. We could ask him for a start if he thought she was still in the Geziret.'

'So we go round the Geziret singing, do we? Bloody hell!'

'We'll have to have an excuse. Or else they'll be jumping on us before we even start.'

'Still hoping, are you, Esmeralda?'

'No, I'm not. I'm just pointing out that if we go round the place singing, a group of posh girls, all nicely dressed up, they'll wonder what the hell is going on.'

'Clap us in prison, most like!'

'Anyway, we ought not to be singing. We ought to be playing our *nays*.'

'But I can't play the *nay*!'

'It's got to be something meaningful. I mean, meaningful to Marie. That's why it has to be the *nay* – I've got it. Why don't we get that dopey *nay* player of hers to do it? She'd recognise him.'

'But would he do it?'

'We could twist his arm.'

'He'd probably do it for love of her, the dope.'

'But where the hell is he? He's not at home, I know that.'

'He's staying at the el Zakis', he's been teaching music to their children. Our cleaner knows the Shawquats and Mrs Shawquat was telling her about it.'

'Staying at the el Zakis'? You mean the Mahmoud el Zakis? The one who's in the Parquet?'

'Yes.'

'Well, I can find that out pretty quickly. My dad's in the Parquet and I know he knows Mahmoud, because I heard him saying so only last week. But how the hell does he come to have a *nay* player staying with him?'

'They're very fond of music, the el Zakis. And not only of music, of the Marie kind of music. Traditional. Not my kind of music, of course, but it's bearable. And just the sort of stuff Marie and her *nay* man would like. Myself, I prefer—'

'Yes, we know what you prefer. But that wouldn't help us: Marie would probably spit if she heard that outside her window. But she wouldn't spit if it was that dopey *nay* player, and she'd recognise him all right.'

At first, Owen dismissed the idea out of hand.

But then he ran into strong internal opposition at the Bab-el-Khalk. Partly because it was an alternative to them walking round the streets themselves; partly because it appealed to that romantic streak in Arabs which is never far under the surface; partly, in Owen's and Mahmoud's view, because it was a tempting alternative to Ali Shawquat's resolution to go to the kidnappers personally and plead with them, and to the strong probability that they would cut his throat; but chiefly, it was down to an unexpected intervention from Mahmoud's wife, Aisha, who apart from not wanting to lose a good music teacher for her children thought that it would work wonders for Ali Shawquat personally.

'It's just what he needs,' she said. 'Something to restore his belief in himself.'

TWELVE

The pavement restaurant was a popular one. It was a centre of activity, with a large crowd gathered round it. Mostly, of course, positioned where it was, they were Kauri boys, and so when a dark-suited, befezzed Effendi joined them, they eyed him askance. They cleared a space for him at the tray, however, and he sat down. When the cook came up, the Effendi pointed to a cut and the cook stabbed it with a spike and plunged it into the fat.

'And what brings you here, Effendi?' asked one of the men squatting nearby. 'You're not from these parts.'

'Just passing through,' said the Effendi. 'But when I saw the company, I said to myself: "They look as if they know what they're doing. The food must be good here!" And suddenly I felt – you know how you do sometimes – really hungry.'

'In that case you have come to the right place!'

There were mutters of agreement.

'But as to what I am doing, you may not believe it, but I'm hard at work.'

'It looks as if you've found the right job.'

'I think I have. But I'm on my feet a lot.'

'So what is it? Go on, tell us.'

'I'm following up a story.'

'Ah,' said the cook, 'you're a newspaperman, are you?'

'Sort of,' said the newcomer, 'but I'm still working on the story.'

'What's it about?'

'Well,' said Mahmoud, for it was he, 'it starts like this. Some men were sitting at a pavement restaurant very like this one, in fact, and a man went by. And the men at the tray looked up at him and said: "What's he doing here? He is not one of us." "He goes by here every day," said the cook. "Nevertheless," said the someone, "he is not one of us." "He is just going about his business," said the cook, "what's wrong with that?" "I don't like his business. So let's kill him." "Kill him," said one of the men at the tray. "What for?" "I don't like his face." "Well, that's not much of a reason. I don't like yours, but I'm not going to kill you for that!" "Ah, but he's an enemy." "How can he be an enemy, when he walks past every day and never gives anyone a bad word?" "Well, maybe he's not an enemy. But it were good if he were one. So let us kill him.'"

There were cries of protest from around the tray.

'That's unreasonable!'

'Would not his brother seek to avenge him?'

'He would.'

'Then that would be a foolish thing to do.'

'It would,' said Mahmoud. 'But that is what the man would have us do.'

'He is a fool, then!'

'Not completely; for he wants to cause mischief, and that he will certainly do.'

'Who is this man?'

'You tell me.'

'Why should I tell you?'

'Because you sit near him.'

'Who are you?' a man said, beginning to stir. 'Are you a Kewfik?'

'I am neither a Kewfik nor a Kauri and I tell you the story so that you may see it as a man from outside.'

'I don't like this story! It is a bad story.'

'It is a bad story about bad men.'

'We should not listen to him,' said one of the men, beginning to get up.

'Sit down! The story is not finished yet.'

'We have heard enough!'

'Did you not like the story? Is that because you know the men? Recognise yourself?'

'I have heard enough,' said the man, pulling out a knife.

'No knives at my table!' said the cook, striking the man hard with a hot ladle.

The man yelped and dropped his knife.

'Are you the one who killed Hamid?' demanded Mahmoud.

The other men jumped up.

'They are the three,' said Mahmoud.

THIRTEEN

The Shawquat house had been unusually quiet for over a week. Mrs Shawquat's husband had been away on business for several days. What business it was she didn't like to ask these days. Certainly it was not at the stables where he always used to work and where, to the best of her understanding, he was supposed to be working still. But Shawquat came and went and was a pain when he was about the house so she was usually quite glad of his absence.

But Ali was a different matter. Of her four children, he was her only son, which was a source of grief to her and chagrin to her husband. She had always felt closest to him and many were the battles she had fought on his behalf. She had thought at one time that he would follow in his father's footsteps and take up a political line of some sort. But he had shown little sign of that, preferring to spend his time at the college, which in Mrs Shawquat's mind was good. She had always supported his father in his political activities and had looked forward to doing the same for their son. His father had expected him to take that path, looking to him to engage in struggles for the ordinary man. She wouldn't have minded him becoming a stablehand like his father, as it was honest work. It would do, she supposed, although she would have liked him to aspire higher. But all he did was make music, which was not so good – certainly not in his father's eyes, but also not in her own eyes, if she were honest.

She was proud of his talent for music. It was not, perhaps, the talent she would have chosen; but when it became apparent that Ali was strongly gifted in this way, she encouraged him, as mothers do. She was not above going down to the playground after school and listening to him on his *nay* like the older children and, increasingly, quite a few of the men too. The Headmaster had told her that such a gift was bestowed by God and not to be neglected and she had always surreptitiously encouraged it.

Her husband, however, had not. He was a practical man and

thought music just a pastime and not a very fruitful one at that. The technical school was where he'd trained his son's sights. But there he had been disappointed. Ali was as little interested in the technical school as he was in politics. To his father he seemed a loss all round.

Disputes in the Shawquat household grew sharper as Ali set aside his father's wishes and spent every free hour practising on his *nay*. Mrs Shawquat urged him to at least go some way to meeting his father halfway but met defeat. He tried – she was sure, despite what his father said, that he tried – but some force kept pulling him back in the old direction. The rows became even fiercer. Ali showed his father's obduracy in sticking to his guns. He spent more and more time out of the home altogether.

And then there was the question of this girl! How Ali had fallen in with her, Mrs Shawquat did not know! She belonged to a different sphere. Shawquat had told his son that; and his wife had, for once, shared his views enough to reinforce the lesson. But to no avail.

Now Ali did not come home at all and his mother grieved. She continued to fight his battles but with an increasingly sinking heart. When would it end? Where could, as the senior Shawquat demanded of her, it end?

She knew, too, that things were uneasy at the stables. The Kewfiks were not at all happy about Shawquat's politicising. In fact, it had been something of a relief when the old man fell sick and went into hospital. It had given the Shawquat family a brief respite. But she had known it would not last. When old Kewfik got out of hospital he was sure to turn on the man he saw as nothing but a troublemaker. And then where would they be?

She had said this to her husband when he got home, and Shawquat said that the job was not important. It was the work, by which he meant the political work, that counted. He had taken up with some new people whom he was sure would look after him. His work with them was growing. When she asked him what it was, he said it was raising money for the cause. What cause was this? The same cause as it always had been: building a better Egypt.

And now a chance had come up that would give the work an added impetus.

There was every possibility that a new alliance could be made locally, one which would create a new force in the land. Or, at any rate, in Geziret. 'Start small, build big!' he had always said to her. He had put his heart and soul into it, and now it appeared to be coming to fruition! And just at this time, when he was at his busiest, when he needed every moment, his wretched son had become a distracting nuisance and was causing trouble!

Worse than that: he was creating trouble with the Kewfiks, of all people. The very people who had the power to crush him, to end his hopes, all he had been working for. All his work over so many years looked like it would come to nothing, and all because of his *son*, he repeated to himself in anguish. Because of his own son!

Everything seemed suddenly to have turned against him. For one thing there was the matter of the powder. Shawquat had suddenly come upon a large new supply, one which could trans-form the finance – and prospects – of the great cause that he was working on. He had assured the people he worked for that there was enough to enable them to lift their efforts to a whole new level. It would open up – well, who knew what it could lead to? For years he had laboured in obscurity; now, suddenly there was the chance to work on a big scale – who knew, perhaps even a national one! The delicate alliance that he had built up so care-fully, and in the face of so many difficulties, between the Kewfiks and the Kauris would seal it. The two sides together were surely big enough to become a force on the Cairo streets and hence in the city itself. His backers were excited, as new possibilities came within their reach. The vision he had for an independent Egypt was suddenly almost inconceivably close. What had been a dream was now a very possible reality. All this seemed to open up with the new supplies of the drug.

But then there came this stupid business with Hamid. And then, suddenly, things began to go wrong.

Why did the Kauris have to kill the delivery man just now, when they were supposed to be working together? It would destroy any hope of an alliance that would unite the people to come out and march in the streets. That one foolish act dis-rupted the system of supply which he had so carefully set up, and drew the attention of the Mamur Zapt. The police were round all over him. The tension that always existed between the Kauris and the Kewfiks had once again burst open.

And on top of all that, there was the kidnapped girl.

The eyes of the world had turned suddenly on the Geziret. It was as if a great spotlight had suddenly been switched on and trained on him and his doings. Things which hitherto had seemed irrelevant, either because they were not to the purpose or too minor to bother about, suddenly became the subject of everybody's attention. That Kewfik girl had nothing to do with him or his work. Yet she had drawn the attention of even more police to the Geziret, just at a time when he could have done without that. Worse, thanks to his son, it had become something to do with him; thanks to the activities of his son, the police attention was beginning to focus on him personally. He couldn't set it aside or ignore it. Questions were being asked by the Mamur Zapt. And one question led to another.

The fact that they had alerted the Mamur Zapt had not pleased the people he worked for. The British, for some strange reason, seemed to pay a lot of attention to kidnapped girls, and even more attention to drugs and that, as Shawquat's backers had pointed out, meant that they would be turning their attention to political activities which in the past had been managed discreetly, even secretly.

And so now they blamed him, Shawquat!

Everything was beginning to go wrong!

Perhaps all was not yet lost, he told himself. Perhaps the Old Woman would work her wonders and produce a settlement. Perhaps then the work could go on. He buried his head in his hands and groaned.

And then, just at that moment there was a knock on the door. His wife went to answer. When she returned, her face was pale.

'The Mamur Zapt!' she said.

'If it's about the boy . . .' said Shawquat.

'It is not.'

'He is no son of mine. He is a loafer, a waster, a dreamer. And will come to no good!'

'I have not come about him,' said Owen.

'Then?'

'I have come about you.'

'Me? I have done nothing! What have the police against me?'

'Drugs.'

'Drugs? I don't touch them. Never have!'

'But you carry them for others.'

'That is not so! Who has put this upon me?'

'A dead man.'

'A dead man? But—'

'Hamid.'

'Hamid? But he cannot have told you anything! He's dead.'

'Dead men sometimes speak.'

'Look, his death was nothing to do with me. I had no hand in that.'

'He was carrying for you.'

'Occasionally, he carried things for me. But—'

'Drugs.'

'Never!'

'The scentmaker makes them up and then sends them to the stables.'

'To the stables, perhaps, but—'

'Addressed to you. I know, because after Hamid died, someone else stepped in for him. One of my men.'

'Your men?'

'Yes. And I opened the package.'

'I – I—'

'It is no good. I have spoken to the scentmaker, and he says he makes up packages regularly for you. But sends them to you at the stables.'

'The scentmaker is a man of no account!'

'There are others who will speak in his support! Come, your hands were on the package. You may have used Hamid, but it was your hands that received it from him. The scentmaker may have put the package together, but he did it at your direction. And he sent it to you, and what I want to know now is what you then did with it. You do not use them yourself, I think?'

'No. Never.'

'You are a God-fearing man, isn't that so?'

'It is so.'

'And would not take them yourself.'

'I never took for myself.'

'But you passed to others? Is that not so?'

'It is so,' Shawquat said, after a moment.

'Who were they?'

'I – I cannot give their names. I do not know them.'

'You know who you passed them to.'

'He did not give me his name.'

'Come!'

'People at the stables.'

'I don't think so. I have seen what was in the package and it was of fine quality. A man working at the stables could not afford it. So?'

'Others. Yes, others.'

'Who?'

'I cannot tell you.'

'Why not? Because you are afraid?'

'Yes, yes!'

'Who are you afraid of?'

'He is a big man.'

'So am I. His name!'

'Ali Fingari,' said Shawquat reluctantly.

'Ali Fingari? Ali Osman Fingari?'

'No. His father.'

The elder Ali Fingari was, unfortunately, not at home.

'Tell him, I'll wait,' said Owen.

He did not have to wait long because as Ali Fingari was leaving by the back door he was seized by Owen's men. They led him round to the front of the house and in to the mandar'ah where Owen was sitting waiting for him.

'Captain Owen, I protest!'

'I wouldn't bother.'

'I am a man of some consequence. Greater consequence, probably, than you suppose.'

'I know who you are.'

'But you don't know who stands behind me!'

'If you are referring to the Khedive, I have spoken to him already.'

'You have?'

'Yes. As I always do. I am the Khedive's servant. When I act, it is for him.'

'You have already spoken to him?'

'Yes.'

'About – about—?'

'About the ways in which you raise money to fund your political enterprises, yes.'

'But – but – I am a long-standing supporter of the Khedive!'

'And he of you. But that does not mean he supports everything you do. Dealing in drugs, for example.'

'This man – this man who has just been killed—'

'Hamid.'

'Is that his name?'

'The one who carried the drugs on your behalf?'

'Not – not on my behalf. On his own behalf. He looked at this as a way to make money for himself—'

'There are those who say not.'

'But you can never trust these men, Captain Owen.'

'I don't trust anyone. And that includes you. As I told the Khedive.'

'And what did he say?'

'He said it was very wise of me. And that he wishes he had followed the same course himself. But there, he said, he has always been too trusting. Especially of those close to him. He knows in his heart that it is foolish, but he can't not trust those he works with every day. Life would be unbearable otherwise. He realises that people let him down but it is a risk that he feels he has to take. I think he was particularly disappointed in your case.'

'But – but – he knew!'

'He says he didn't.'

'But that's not true!'

'It is your word against his. A Pasha's word against the Khedive's. Guess whose word will count in the end.'

'But – but – that's not fair!'

'Who said that life near the throne was ever fair?'

'But—'

'What we have to do now, I think, is to sit down – here, in this beautiful room, will do; the alternative is the Bab-el-Khalk

– and talk quietly, as two friends – as we are friends, are we not? And we shall see if we can get somewhere, without necessarily having to have recourse to the Courts. The legal one, of course, is what I am talking about.'

Ali Fingari swallowed.

'And if I – if I talk now, here, as you suggest, would that mean I would not have to talk in the Courts? The legal ones, that is?'

'It depends on the Khedive. And, naturally, he is a man to be trusted.'

'What is it you want to know?'

What Owen wanted to know was how far the political dealing and drug dealing went. At a place like the Egyptian Royal Court, in those days, there was always manoeuvring, not least by the Khedive himself. But Owen always liked to keep up to date with the manoeuvres. Then he could contain them. Containment was what he was after. Getting rid of them altogether was out of the question. He suspected that Whitehall was just the same. It was the way of the world.

Ali Fingari spilled all. And then Owen left him quietly to stew at home until, with the Khedive, he could decide what to do with him.

'I am shocked!' said the younger Ali Osman Fingari. 'More than shocked: deeply hurt! To think that my old man was setting me up so that I would carry the can while he would get off scot-free if anything went wrong, well, it's outrageous. I have a suspicion that he thought things were about to go wrong and that's why he was getting out of the way. And leaving me in it, the scoundrel! And all the time he pretends he had no money and leaves me to carry *that* can too!'

'Of course, by the time all this ends it will probably be the truth,' said Owen. 'Your father will be left with no money.'

'And what about me?' asked Osman anxiously.

'Well . . .'

'Don't tell me! It will all be gone again. Only the Khedive will have it this time!'

It had seemed a good idea at the time, when Layla had propounded it in the classroom. In the colder light of day, however, problems arose. Mostly they were practical problems. First, there was the question of the *nay* itself. It was a flute-like instrument made originally from a single reed and blown. Everyone was familiar with it – it was probably the most common instrument of them all – but how far would the sound carry? Would it be lost in the street or would it reach into the houses, where, after all, Marie was likely to be? Illumination was sought from Ali Shawquat, who was not only a player himself of much experience but also the one who was most likely to be playing it on the day. He said that the way he would play it on this occasion would penetrate through walls of iron and doors of brass. Owen was not entirely reassured but let it go.

No, for Ali the problem was not how he should play it but where he should play it. Somewhere in the Geziret, no doubt, but the Geziret was a big district: where precisely?

They didn't have to be too precise about it, Layla said: Ali Shawquat was prepared to play his *nay* on behalf of his beloved anywhere. He would play all day, he would, he swore, cover every inch of the Geziret. If the *nay* could be heard, it would be heard. In its favour was the fact that the Geziret was a poor quarter through which there was little traffic. Admittedly, the traffic would consist only of donkeys, camels and the occasional cart or even more occasional horse-drawn arabeah. Arabeahs were the taxi of Cairo, but in the Geziret there was not much call for taxis. In the Geziret the *nay*'s sound would travel through and into the houses with ease. Besides, where they had doors, the doors would be open. It would be rather, said McPhee in an unfortunate comparison, like the Pied Piper of Hamelin: the rats, or in this case, the inhabitants of the Geziret would come running.

Owen was still not convinced and asked Ali Shawquat if he could identify more accurately the places where the kidnappers were likely to be found. He couldn't. His mind had been on other things, and he had not taken it in.

Owen's next intended port of call was the instrument repair shop, where so many of the Geziret musical instruments went for repair, but on his way there he remembered that he might have a more immediate source of information in Ali Shawquat's friend, an *'ood* player himself. And now he remembered the *'ood* player's wife, with whom he had spoken before, and who had seemed sympathetic. He went to see her. She was preoccupied with her baby on her knee. Once again her husband was not there.

The wife remembered him and went to back away, but he reminded her of Marie and her plight. Her curiosity re-aroused, the wife came forward again. But, she said, she couldn't help. She knew nothing about it and her husband wouldn't like it. This was the Geziret, she said.

Owen said that he quite understood and would not press her; but he did wonder if she could help in a general way, seeing that the fate of a fellow woman was at stake.

'Well . . .' she said, looking at him doubtfully.

After some thought, and swearing her to silence, he spoke of the girls' plan. He told her about Ali Shawquat going round the Geziret, forlornly playing his *nay* and hoping to hear an echo.

'She would hear the *nay*,' she said, 'and know that it was his *nay*.'

'And would find a way of signalling back,' said Owen.

'How?' said the wife doubtfully.

'That is the question. We thought she might sing in response. She and Ali often used to sing together. Him playing the nay, she singing. There are songs, Ali said, that she would know, and he would play those.'

'It would be as in the old stories,' she breathed, her eyes shining.

'As in the old stories,' said Owen.

'And she the lady in the tower!'

'Pining for her lover,' said Owen.

'Yes!' said the wife, far away. 'Yes!'

'All they need is a little help,' said Owen.

She shrank away.

'I cannot!' she said. 'I cannot.'

'A clue is all they ask,' said Owen. 'Which area should he play in? The *nay* player's feet will walk all day, but the Geziret is large. Cannot you give him a hint where he should play?'

'My husband would kill me,' she whispered.

'He will never know.'

'Even my husband does not know where they keep her. After you came before, I asked him. But he said he did not know.'

'The sound would travel through the streets. We do not need to know where exactly. But put us within reach of the woman, that she may hear, and within reach of the voice so that if she replies we will hear that too.'

'I – I dare not.'

'It is a woman that needs your help. What sort of woman is it that cannot help another woman when she is in need?'

A broken sob came from behind the face veil.

'Take me to the area. I do not need to know the place exactly.'

'I do not know it exactly!'

'But you know roughly where. Lead me there and stand. And then walk away, that is all I ask.'

'They will hurt her.'

'I shall move very quickly when the time comes. I would not ask, but I think this is our last chance. It depends on you. Cannot you help at least a little? As one woman for another?'

She stood there wavering for some time and he thought he had lost her. But then she made up her mind.

'Follow,' she said. 'But not too closely.'

She started off along the narrow, dirty street, her baby in her arms. He waited and then followed, but on the other side of the street, and looking up at the buildings as if in search of a particular one. In his fez and a not particularly smart suit, he might have been a lowly official.

It helped that the street was an old one, the woodwork was faded, the mud-brick walls crumbling, but the houses had character. The windows were meshrebiya and if you looked closely you saw that the lattice work was fine. He peered at it as he walked along, scrutinising the craftsmanship.

He came to a small *sebil*, or fountain house, with delicate stone tracery and looping arabesques. Inscriptions were carved into the dark masonry. The fountain chamber itself was lined with beautiful old blue tiles. He stopped for a moment to study it. From the *kuttub*, the small school, upstairs he could hear children's voices. They had a clear, bell-like quality which reached out through the tops of the houses.

The woman walked on, through ever-narrowing streets. The houses leant across overhead almost touching the ones on the opposite side of the street, giving shade from the sun and shelter from the heat. Some of the box-like window frames jutted out so far as almost to be built into the house opposite.

The wife turned sharply into an opening so small that it could easily have been missed. The street itself would hardly have taken a donkey. In fact, there was a camel coming the other way towards them carrying a large load of *berseem*, or clover, for feeding the carriage animals. The load stretched out on both sides, scraping walls, until finally they stuck. The driver tried to get the camel to go back but camels don't retreat easily and there was a lot of time lost before the manoeuvre succeeded. Just when it seemed that all was well, the camel came to an obstacle and stopped again.

This time it was a beggar squatting in the street. He was blind and in his hand he held an *'ood*, that lute-like musical instrument, which he was proposing to play. A small boy with a tin bowl stood beside him. The beggar struck up a tune and the small boy began to sing not very well.

The camel driver cursed and there was some argument before the beggar rose reluctantly to his feet and moved away.

The woman with her baby turned up an even narrower alley and then stopped. Owen came up behind her and almost bumped into her. As he bent near to her apologising she said softly: 'Somewhere around here. I don't know where.'

She moved away and then said, even more quietly: 'God go with you! And with my sister,' she added, as she moved off.

That part of the Geziret was a warren. It did not consist of streets or even alley ways but of passages, many of which led into one another. With a sinking heart he realised that he would never be able to place his men where he wanted. He had taken careful note of the way he had come but had no larger mental picture of the area, much less, of course, of where Marie actually was.

The next day he returned with the *nay* player and they began to work their way through the area. Owen made a particular point of going to the *sebil* again, pretending to be studying the inscriptions. Above them he could hear again the sound of the children's voices. They carried well, even in this crowded, built-up area.

Could he not use that in some way?

At the end of the day he met up with the *nay* player and they compared notes.

'My voice isn't right. It is too low. It needs to be – like the children's voices in the *kuttub*.'

'Let's get some children, then.'

The next morning the *nay* player brought several and tested their voices before setting out. Some had come from the senior forms at the Khedivial and Layla had come with them. Her own voice, as the *nay* player pointed out, wouldn't do. It was too full, too low, too womanly. 'Like Marie's.'

'I'll get some juniors,' said Layla.

The next morning, true to her word, she brought several. Minya was among them.

'I'm afraid not,' said Owen gently. 'Your Headmistress wouldn't like it.'

Minya stuck her lip out and pouted.

'That's not fair,' she said. 'I'm a good singer.'

'She is,' said the *nay* player unexpectedly. 'Just right!'

'There you are!' said Minya. 'And she would know my voice. She made me practise my singing as we walked to school.'

'If you were bigger,' said Owen.

'My voice would be different then,' said Minya. 'At the moment, it's just right.'

'It is,' said the *nay* player.

'No,' said Owen.

'I will go with her,' said Layla.

'No,' said Owen.

'It is just right!' said the *nay* player.

'Selim could go with me,' said Minya.

'A policeman wouldn't look right,' said Owen.

'He could dress differently,' said Minya.

'He could bring her to me,' said the *nay* player. 'And then just stand there chatting. People do.'

'Well . . .'

'Selim is a very good chatter,' said Minya.

'Well, all right,' said Owen. 'We'll give it a go.'

Later in the morning the *nay* player took up position. And later still Selim came along with Minya. Minya exuding determination at every pore.

'Listen to the rhythm,' ordered the *nay* player. 'Sing to the *nay*.'

'I will,' promised Minya. 'And to Marie,' she added softly to herself.

The *nay* player smiled.

'And I will do the same,' he said. 'And perhaps between the two of us . . .'

They sang all through the morning. In the heat even Selim began to wilt. The *nay* player sent him to the fountain house to get some water. He had just returned when from one of the houses nearby a girl's voice began to answer.

'It's Marie!' cried Minya.

FOURTEEN

Selim rushed past Owen and ran up the narrow staircase. At the top two men were standing, bewildered, Selim barrelled through them – at least, that was what he must have done. To Owen at the time it appeared that he had simply run over them. They fell back and down the stairs into the arms of Owen's men coming in. Selim charged on. The door at the top was closed, possibly locked. Selim crashed through it. Two more men inside looked up amazed. Something happened to them and they fell heavily against the wall. On the other side of the room a startled Marie was standing by the window. Selim scooped her up and ran downstairs, to where Minya and the *nay* player were waiting for her.

'I knew it was your voice!' said a tearful, delighted Marie.

'Oh, I'm so glad!' said Minya. 'I sang my best, I really did!'

'You were perfect!' said the *nay* player.

'Was I, really?' said Minya, turning pink beneath her tan.

'This time I did not run away!' said the *nay* player.

'You didn't!' said Marie, hugging him. 'And you didn't before. You were just taken by surprise.'

'Get them out of here,' Owen ordered his men. He didn't want any last-minute difficulties.

'And thank you, Minya,' he said, looking down to where an ecstatic Minya stood holding Selim's hand. 'Him, too,' said Owen. 'All of you. Back to the Bab-el-Khalk!'

Georgiades slipped into the room.

'And now the money,' he said to the kidnappers they were holding. 'Where is it?'

'Ahmet has it,' they said sullenly.

'And where is Ahmet?'

'Over here, Effendi. I was told to keep it safe.'

'And have you kept it safe?'

'Of course, Effendi! What do you think I am? A thief?'

'I want it here, in my hands.'

'Certainly, Effendi. I will go and fetch it.'

'And in case of accidents,' said Georgiades 'I will come with you.'

'Of course, Effendi,' said Ahmet, looking rather cast down.

'And I will count,' said Nikos, coming in just at that moment. Nikos trusted neither the kidnappers nor Georgiades. Not that he doubted Georgiades's honesty, it was his ability to count that he distrusted.

So relieved was Nikos at the prospect of returning to home ground at the Bab-el-Khalk that he overcame his fears about speaking to little girls and offered to buy Minya an ice cream. Georgiades asked if he could have one too. And Minya asked if Selim could also have one. Stretching several points, and growing increasingly relieved as they approached the Bab-el-Khalk, Nikos agreed, and even went so far as to pat Minya on the head.

Back at the Bab-el-Khalk, Layla, who had been pacing up and down, threw her arms around Marie and both girls collapsed, sobbing.

'It was Layla's idea,' said Owen.

'As acting head of the family,' said Ali Osman, 'I feel a certain responsibility for the girl.'

'I'm glad you do,' said Owen.

Ali Osman hung his head.

'I've not done very well so far,' he acknowledged.

'You will learn.'

'I hope so,' said Ali Osman. 'By the way, now that the ransom doesn't have to be paid, there must be some money floating around?'

'I gather the bank is seeing to that,' said Owen.

'I – I have never found them very helpful,' said Osman. 'I was wondering if you could put in a word . . .'

'Glad to,' said Owen. 'But I'm afraid that the way things are, I shall have to put in quite a lot of words.'

'Necessary, I'm sure,' said Ali Osman.

'Well, actually, I hope not. Marie's father is recovering and will soon be able to resume his responsibilities.'

'He shouldn't resume them too quickly,' said Osman hastily. 'Not after his serious illness.'

'True. But fortunately he has his wife to lean on, and now that she has Marie back with her, you'll be surprised at the difference in her.'

'Nevertheless, on financial matters . . .' said Ali Osman.

'The bank is helping.'

'Glad to hear it,' said Ali Osman, if a trifle sadly. 'And, of course she will need advice on the girl. After all that she has been through . . .'

'Fortunately, her mother is the sister of one of the Khedive's wives, who has promised to help.'

'Oh, good!' said Ali Osman, disappointed.

'The trickiest bit is still the old difficulty,' said Owen.

'Old difficulty?'

'The daughter is even more in love with the *nay* player.'

'A *nay* player? Quite unsuitable!'

'But they do love each other.'

'What has that got to do with it?'

'I am sure,' said Owen, 'that a man like you, with all your wealth of international experience, will be aware that things are changing. Particularly among the young who, increasingly, are adopting the view that love should play a part in marriage.'

'Well, naturally,' said Ali Osman. 'I have always been of the view that a wife should love her husband.'

'So that seems all right then,' said Owen.

'All right?' said Ali Osman hesitating.

'So far as the relationship with the *nay* player is concerned.'

'Well, yes. I mean, but there are two sides to this. If not three. Surely the father has a voice in this?'

'In my experience, fathers always counsel delay.'

'Wisely!' said Ali Osman.

'But their daughters usually prevail.'

'I am all for listening to the wisdom of the aged,' said Ali Osman.

'Your father, for instance?'

'Naturally, there are exceptions.'

'As I said, Marie's father is increasingly coming to the view that Marie may have it right. He is a bit of a romantic, is old Kewfik, especially now that he has recovered his daughter, and the idea of the *nay* player singing for her tickles his fancy.

And his wife is thrilled to bits. As for the boy's father, old Shawquat, well, he is not in a position to say anything. So I think the wedding will go ahead.'

'The foolishness of the young!' said Ali Osman ruefully.

'They realise that they will have no money. A *nay* player, even a good one, has to scrape to earn a living. But they both feel, Ali and Marie, that they can make a go of it.'

'Ah, the young!' said Ali Osman, shaking his head.

Ali Shawquat's mother was actually quite pleased at the proposal of a new daughter-in-law. She had initially taken the side of her husband, feeling that Marie was too exalted to sit comfortably in a yoke with her own very dear but also, she thought privately, rather foolish son. *Nay* playing was all very well but – but, as she told herself, how would they have located the kidnapped Marie if it had not been for the *nay* playing?

She put this to her husband.

'I hope it works for me too,' said the elder Shawquat, 'when I am in the *caracol.*'

'They told me you'll be there for some time,' she said to her husband. 'And by the time you get out, I may be the grand-mother of a darling boy. Moreover, with more women in the family, no one is going to listen to you, old man!'

'Discourage him from becoming a *nay* player,' said her intransigent husband.

'Why?' said Marie.

'Why?' said his wife.

'Why?' said Ali Shawquat Junior, who had grown greatly more mature of late. Aisha's gentle tutoring may have had something to do with this, together with Ali's delight at being able to share the mystery of the *nay* with her children, who both continued to take to his lessons well. Aisha was reluctant to part with an in-house *nay* player. Not many people, as she observed, had one. The Mahmoud and Aisha household had always inclined to the musical, and now it positively filled with music, much to Mahmoud's delight. Particularly when Ali invited round his old friend the awalim and she sang to his *nay*.

The house soon became the centre of a little musical world which became quite famous in Cairo for favouring the old songs.

All sorts of people came to it, including the Old Woman of the souk and even, on occasion, the Mamur Zapt. Minya came to the house regularly and, singing so often with a top-class *nay* player and a really distinguished exponent of the art of the awalim, gradually became a well-known singer herself. Girls from the Khedivial started dropping in and the popularity of the old songs grew into a major movement.